Kathy Helidoniotis

Horse
MAD
academy

HORSE MAD
3

Angus&Robertson
An imprint of HarperCollins*Publishers*

Angus&Robertson
An imprint of HarperCollins*Publishers*

First published in 2006
by HarperCollins*Publishers* Australia Pty Limited
ABN 36 009 913 517
www.harpercollins.com.au

HarperCollins*Publishers*
25 Ryde Road, Pymble, Sydney NSW 2073, Australia
31 View Road, Glenfield, Auckland 0627, New Zealand
1–A, Hamilton House, Connaught Place, New Delhi – 110 001, India
77–85 Fulham Palace Road, London W6 8JB, United Kingdom
2 Bloor Street East, 20th floor, Toronto, Ontario M4W 1A8, Canada
10 East 53rd Street, New York NY 10022, USA

National Library of Australia Cataloguing-in-Publication data:

Helidoniotis, Kathy.
    Horse mad academy.
    For children aged 8+.
    ISBN 13: 978 0 7322 8422 0.
    ISBN 10: 0 7322 8422 8.
    1. Horses – Juvenile fiction. I. Title.
    (Series: Helidoniotis, Kathy. Horse mad; bk. 3).
A823.4

Cover design by Darren Holt, HarperCollins Design Studio
Cover photography by Belinda Taylor, www.bellaphotoart.com.au
Art direction and stylist: Christine Orchard
Typeset in Bembo 13/18pt by Kirby Jones
Printed and bound in Australia by Griffin Press

60gsm Bulky Paperback used by HarperCollins*Publishers* is a natural,
recyclable product made from wood grown in a combination of sustainable
plantation and regrowth forests. The manufacturing processes conform to
the environmental regulations in Tasmania, the place of manufacture.

9 8 7 6 5 4   08 09 10 11 12

For Mariana, John and Simon,
with love.

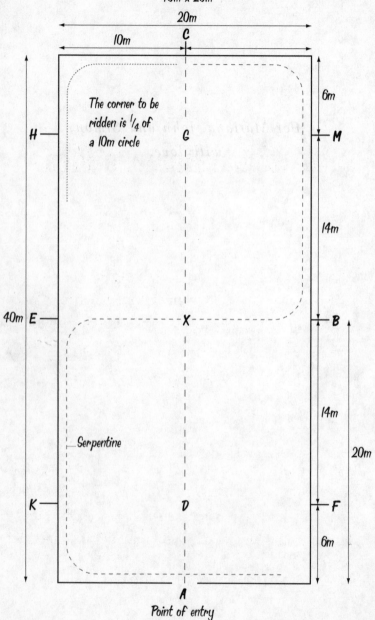

SMALL DRESSAGE ARENA
40m x 20m

20m

10m

C

The corner to be ridden is ⅟₄ of a 10m circle

6m

H

G

M

14m

40m E

X

B

40m

14m

20m

Serpentine

K

D

F

6m

A

Point of entry

ONE

A Girl, a Horse, a Flea

'Take a good look, Honey,' I murmured.

My gorgeous chestnut mare tossed her head and snorted. I sat on her bare back in our paddock, trying to commit every sight, sound and smell to memory. After all, we were going to be away from Shady Creek for four whole weeks. I was going to miss home so much!

Honey's smooth back was warm beneath me. My legs hung freely at her sides. I loved to sit like this, the two of us as close as we could be. No saddle, no blanket, nothing separating us from each other. Honey is the love of my life. I couldn't imagine life without her.

I fidgeted with my reins and gazed around me. A year ago I was living in the city in a tiny house, with an even tinier backyard, riding once a week and dreaming that some day I would have a horse of my own. And now here I was in Shady Creek.

The events of the year marched through my head one after the other like a spectacular, noisy parade. Leaving the city and almost losing Jenna, my best friend. Starting at a new school and meeting Becky. Finding Honey and rescuing her from her cruel owners. Joining Shady Creek Riding Club and riding in the gymkhana. Jenna coming to stay. The Championships. And now there was a new baby on the way!

'Hang on tight, Spiller!' A voice taunted me from across the paddock.

'Take a bath, Fleabag!' I hollered back.

The only thing I hate about Shady Creek are the Three Creepketeers — Flea Fowler, Carly Barnes and Ryan Thomas from Riding Club. They have one goal in life — to make my life, and Becky's, miserable. Unfortunately, Flea is a whole lot closer than I'd like him to be — he lives right smack bang next door to me. And his favourite form of entertainment is watching me ride Honey, just in case I fall off.

'Aren't you s'posed to have gone by now?' Carly shrieked.

I could just make them out through the trees. Flea was grooming his wicked pure black gelding, Scud, his hair sticking up all over the place in its trademark 'infested by a family of ferrets' style, while Carly looked on. Scud is the only horse I've ever had a hate-hate relationship with. He threw me into a blackberry bush on my first day in Shady Creek, earning me the nickname Spiller Miller, which I despise.

'Believe me I can't wait!' I bawled. 'The further away I get from you two the better.'

Flea and Carly cackled, unperturbed. I drummed my heels against Honey's sides and she ambled across the paddock towards the house.

'Just think, Honey,' I said, their horrible screeching laughter ringing in my ears. 'Four whole entire Creep-free weeks. It'll be like a little taste of heaven.'

I rode my Honey horse into her corral, threw my right leg over her shoulder and slid to the ground. We had a float to catch!

TWO

Waratah Grove
Riding Academy

'This is awesome!'

I stood in the float parking area of Waratah Grove Riding Academy and gaped open-mouthed at my surroundings.

'Don't let any flies in, Ash,' Mum said, squeezing out of the car. She was really pregnant now and strongly resembled a feed bin on legs. 'Grant, where's the loo?'

'How would Dad know?' I moaned. I couldn't believe how often she needed to find a loo. It was practically a full-time job. Come to think of it, being

4

a plumber, it was her job. In fact, she'd spent the last few weeks trying to convince Dad that we needed to install a toilet in every room of the house.

A pained expression crossed Mum's face. Dad leapt to her side, pushing me out of the way. I scowled and dusted myself off. For a nurse, surrounded by sick people day in, day out, he was not coping well with Mum's pregnancy. One of her favourite stories is how Dad fainted when I was born and all the midwives rushed around him and left her all alone with me sticky and red with a scrunched-up face.

'What is it, Helen? What's wrong? Is the baby okay? Are you okay? I'll get the blood pressure machine out of the boot. Thank goodness I packed it!' he said without stopping to draw a breath. He was definitely taking this pregnancy thing a bit too far. He'd even had worse morning sickness than Mum.

She smiled and touched his face tenderly with her fingertips. Yuck!

'It's nothing to worry about, really. It's just that we've been driving for hours and this baby is treating my bladder like a trampoline. Complete with double backflips.'

'Ash, will you be —' Dad began.

'Just go,' I said sourly. 'Don't worry about me. It's only my first day at Waratah Grove Riding Academy. I'll be fine here all by myself while you two . . . '

But they'd already wandered off in search of the toilets. What kind of parents were they anyway? I was sick of this baby. All I ever heard was baby this and baby that. Sure it had been fun for a while, like the time Mum had let me put my ear on her tummy to listen to the baby's heartbeat. But then the baby kicked me square in the face. Not even born yet and already bossing me around and beating me up! Becky was right. So was Jenna. Siblings stank!

Just when I was really starting to feel sorry for myself a horse neighed loudly. I shook my head and rubbed my eyes. It was like waking up from a dream (an especially bad one about mums who always need to go to the loo and dads who ignore their precious firstborn daughters).

I was at Waratah Grove! One of the best riding academies in the country, maybe even in the Southern Hemisphere. I'd wanted to come here since forever and here I was standing on what could only be described as hallowed ground.

I spun around slowly on the spot, taking everything in. The float parking area was perfect and clean with a white fence and stylish steel drinking troughs installed in each corner. There was a huge stone statue of a sleek black horse in the centre, springing from a garden of fat red roses. The waiting area was part of a series of horseshoe-shaped immaculate riding rings, tall viewing stands and stables. Behind the rings I could see a huge red ranch-style home. All around me well-dressed kids were backing their horses down the ramps of gleaming horse floats, parents were fussing and suitcases were being piled onto a long silver trolley. Horses, some in brightly coloured rugs and travel boots, were being led into the stables one by one. Their hooves clip-clopped on the cobblestones. Chatter, laughter and whinnying washed over me. It was the closest I'd come to horse-lovers' heaven and made the facilities at Shady Creek Riding Club look like a pair of scungy old thongs next to a brand spanking new pair of RM Williams boots.

Something caught my eye. A streak of silver was being backed out of the float parked beside us. I gasped. I'd never seen such a wonderful horse. Her coat was truly silver and glittered in the sunlight. Her mane and tail moved like running water and her legs were fine but strong. Her dark brown eyes were gentle, watching the rushed goings-on around her with a mixture of curiosity and calm. Her dished face had the look of an Arab. I'd always wanted an Arab. I wondered who her rider was as I scanned the crowd for suspects. I made up my mind then and there to meet whoever it was and, hopefully, become friends. Anyone who owned a horse like that was okay in my books.

I heard shuffling in our float (borrowed just for today from Gary Cho) and was jolted back to reality. Honey! I wriggled the bolts on the ramp of the float until they slid out. I lowered the ramp and noticed that Honey had left a present for me.

'You've been busy,' I said to her as I climbed up the ramp and wrenched open the boom. Honey snorted in agreement. I jumped down and skipped to the side door of the float, unlocked it and climbed inside. Honey was pleased to see me. She shook her head and pulled back on her lead rope.

'Okay, okay,' I murmured, undoing the knot in her lead. 'I know, I left you in here too long. I'm sorry I was just so … It's just … Oh you'll see for yourself.'

With Honey's lead rope in my hand I ducked under the bar and gave her chest a gentle push. She backed down the ramp slowly and emerged into the sunlight.

'That's better.' A very relieved-looking Mum and her belly were waiting. Dad hovered behind her.

'Ashleigh Miller!'

I spun around, clutching Honey's lead and came face to face with a tall woman whose grey hair was twisted into a roll on top of her head. The green tartan knickerbockers were gone but there was no mistaking her.

'Mrs Strickland,' I said.

'Hello, Miss Miller.' Mrs Strickland grabbed my free hand and pumped it vigorously, then slapped Honey's neck. 'Hello, Honey.'

I beamed at her. She was such a sweet old lady. She remembered Honey!

'This is my mum and dad,' I said.

Mrs Strickland shook their hands. 'We've been looking forward to seeing Miss Miller at Waratah

Grove again. Her ride at the Championships was quite impressive.'

Dad nudged me and grinned, wiggling his eyebrows. I gave him a look. It was going to take more than one of his famous eyebrow dances to win me back.

'If you'd care to join us.' Mrs Strickland indicated a large group of riders waiting near the statue.

'Sure!' I beamed. 'Right away. Can't wait!'

A young man with a piece of straw wedged between his top and bottom teeth and very tanned skin was leaning on the silver trolley I'd seen earlier. He poked at my bags with the toe of his boot and pushed his hair out of his eyes. 'Can I take these for you?'

'Yes, please.'

He held his hand out. 'I think I'd better take her for you first, though. Who is this?'

I handed him Honey's lead. I would never hand her over to just anybody, but he looked like someone I could trust. I could see it in his eyes. This was a horsy kind of guy. 'Her name's Honey. Honey Miller.'

He nodded. 'Cross-country, right?'

It was my turn to nod.

'Stall thirteen.'

'Thirteen?' I grimaced, hoping that centuries of superstition were about to be turned on their ears. The young man smiled knowingly.

'Don't worry. We've had a long line of champions in stall thirteen. The last horse we had in there was Ivory Queen.'

'Ivory Queen. Wow!' Ivory Queen had just placed second overall in the Australian National Three-Day Event Championships. And Honey was going to be in her stall. I felt star-struck!

The young man led Honey away towards the stables.

I jogged over to the group of waiting riders. I stood next to a girl about my age whose dark brown hair hung past her shoulders in spiral curls. She was all decked out in pink — from head to foot. The collar and lapels of her jacket were decorated with fine floaty white feathers that danced about whether she moved or not. I smiled at her. She smiled back. Everybody was so friendly! The next four weeks were going to be like one long beautiful horse mad dream. I was going to love it here. I was never going to want to leave. I was going to quit school and live here in heaven (aka Waratah Grove) and be the youngest rider ever to compete for Australia at the Olympic Games and they would build a statue of me right next to that one of the gorgeous black horse and . . .

Mrs Strickland cleared her throat. I shook my head and the daydream evaporated like rain on a corrugated iron roof in February. We all looked up at her.

'Good day and welcome,' she said. 'Welcome to all those who are returning and those who are joining us for the first time. Our first item of business today is lunch, so if all riders and parents will follow me to our dining room, we'll be happy to serve you.'

I trooped out of the waiting area with the mob of riders, turning to grin at my parents (okay, I was sort of starting to forgive them). We went through a gate that led to a corridor, which ran between two riding rings, then past the red ranch house and up some stairs to the dining room. We jostled our way through the door, everybody wanting to be first. The dining room was like nothing I'd ever seen before in the horsy world. Sure there were the usual tables and benchs. But the walls! They were decorated with trophies, certificates, photos, newspaper clippings, and portraits of horses. I use the term 'decorated', but wallpapered is much more accurate. Every square centimetre of wall was covered with news of riders who'd attended Waratah Grove.

Mrs Strickland pointed at a buffet loaded with food and drinks, and the riders swarmed towards it like hungry ponies to a clover patch. Mum and Dad made their way through the crowd (actually, the crowd seemed to part for Mum like the Red Sea parted for Moses) and we loaded our plates with roast potatoes, salad, long green beans with butter and spicy chicken drumsticks. My mouth was watering. I hadn't realised how hungry I was. We settled at a table by a huge window.

'This is great, Ash,' Dad mumbled through a mouthful of roast potato.

I winced. 'Haven't you always told me not to speak with my mouth full?'

Dad swallowed and took a long drink of water. 'Yeah, but this food is fantastic. When I was a kid we were lucky to get stale bread and dripping at camp. If you eat like this every day, Honey won't be able to hold you up!'

Dad speared a piece of chicken and gobbled it. Mum watched him wistfully.

'Not hungry?' I asked. She'd barely touched her lunch.

'Indigestion,' she grumbled. 'But at this stage I can't tell if it's the baby squeezing the stuffing out of my stomach or your father's story. He's never eaten dripping in his life.'

I frowned. Here we go. The baby. Couldn't we have one conversation without talking about the baby? I was positive they'd forget my name once the baby finally was born. I might have to wear a name tag in the house and even then they'll probably look at me and think, 'How did that kid with the riding boots on get in here again?'

Dad scooped up some beans, shrugged and gave me a wink before starting on Mum's lunch.

Soon after the dining hall fell silent and I looked around to see what was going on. Mrs Strickland was standing on a small stage, sending a rather annoyed look in the direction of our table. The other riders and their parents had finished eating and were watching her politely. I gave Dad's leg a kick under the table.

'Ow! What the devil did you do that for?' Dad pointed his fork at me. A huge wedge of tomato fell splat onto the table.

'Dad,' I hissed, hot-faced. 'Everyone's looking.'

'I think we're in trouble!' Dad whispered, wiping his mouth with a paper serviette.

Mrs Strickland nodded at us. 'Thank you.'

I wanted to disappear. Do parents go to some sort of school to learn how to be embarrassing or does it just happen naturally?

'I'd like to take this opportunity to once again welcome your children to Waratah Grove.' Mrs Strickland smoothed her tweed jacket and tucked a stray wisp of hair behind her ear. 'I really should say *our* children. Once a rider has passed through our Academy they become a part of the Waratah Grove family.'

I looked around the room. Most of the parents were smiling and nodding. Some of the kids looked terrified. The pink girl with the spiral curls was chewing loudly on a huge wad of pink bubble gum.

Mrs Strickland continued. 'Now, I would like you to take the opportunity to say goodbye to your children and leave via the door we entered. Our students will remain here to receive further instruction.'

Mum gasped. So did I. Now that they had to leave, they didn't seem all that bad. Even if all they talked about was the baby. I realised suddenly that I'd never been away from home before. Three overnighters at Grade 5 camps didn't count in the face of four whole weeks. And at least at camp I'd always had Jenna. But I didn't know anybody here except for Mrs Strickland and I doubted she'd be wanting me to sleep on a fold-out bed in her room for the next month. Terror gripped me. I felt the spicy chicken drumsticks rolling around my stomach. This was not a good feeling. Not good at all.

'Thank you for making the journey and we look forward to seeing you at graduation in four weeks' time.'

Graduation? What was this, school?

Mrs Strickland climbed down from the stage and immediately began shooing parents out of the room. Everyone started talking at once. I grabbed Mum's hand. I didn't want her to leave.

Dad gave me a quick cuddle and smooshed my

cheek with a bristly kiss. 'We'll be here for graduation and call us anytime.'

'And email or write,' Mum added, heaving herself off the bench. 'Ooh, my backside hurts.'

'What's wrong? It could be early labour. Do you have cramps? *Do you have cramps?*' Dad was turning purple.

'Oh for heaven's sake, Grant, I've been sitting on a wooden bench.' Mum looked at me, smiling and rubbing her built-in soccer ball. 'You be careful, Ash. And make some nice friends.'

'And make sure you eat well and ride safely. No monkey business!' Dad frowned, squeezing my other hand.

'And write to Gran, she bought you that nice stationery set, don't forget. And Uncle Bill, too.'

I held their hands and smiled weakly. 'Don't worry. Honey will take care of me,' I said, hoping I sounded a whole lot happier than I felt.

Dad smiled, drawing me into another warm hug. 'I'm sure she will.'

Mum did a strange bounce all of a sudden. 'Grant, I need the ....'

'Just concentrate on your breathing.' He slipped his arm around her shoulder, panting like a dog in the midday sun.

'Just go,' I croaked. 'I'll be okay.'

Mrs Strickland was getting closer. Most of the parents were now gone.

'Go,' I said again.

Mum grabbed my shoulders and pulled me close — well as close as she could with all that baby in the way.

'I love you, possum,' she whispered. I squeezed her back and broke away, my eyes stinging.

I looked around the room at the other riders. They were grouping at the tables closest to the stage, which Mrs Strickland had been standing on earlier. Plates clattered as they were being collected. I crossed the room and sat on a bench at the end of one of the tables.

'Shove up a bit, will ya?'

I turned quickly to see who it was. The girl with the long brown spiral curls was sitting next to me, a huge smile on her face. Now that she was so close I realised that she was wearing make-up. Her lips were painted thickly with pink lipstick, her eyes were smeared with blue and black stuff and there were gold sparkles on her cheeks.

I shuffled along the bench. A second girl with short hair, so fair it was almost white, neat riding clothes and a dusting of freckles on her upturned nose squeezed in next to Spiral Curls.

'First time?' Spiral Curls asked.

I nodded.

'You'll have a great time, it's, like, *so* much fun here.' Spiral Curls chewed on her bubble gum and smiled.

I smiled back, relieved.

'I'm Ashleigh,' I said, holding out my hand. 'Ashleigh Miller.'

'I've heard all about you,' Spiral Curls said, shaking my hand. Her fingernails were long and painted pink to match her lips. I glanced quickly at my own nails, which were short and painted with this morning's horse grime. Just the way I liked it. 'Juliette and I were just talking about you.'

I was surprised. 'You were?'

Spiral Curls patted my knee. 'We remember you from the cross-country. Awesome riding. We, like, haven't stopped talking about it. It's so good to meet you face to face. I can just tell we're gonna be, like, *such* good friends. Right, Juliette?'

The girl with short white hair nodded. 'Good friends.'

'I hope we're in the same cabin. That would be, like, *so* cool.' Spiral Curls flicked her hair around a bit.

'So cool,' Juliette said.

'Cool,' I said, beaming at them. My first impression of the riders was totally one hundred per cent accurate. They were so friendly!

Somebody clapped their hands twice and there was silence. Even Spiral Curls stopped talking. Mrs Strickland climbed up onto the stage. We all looked up at her. She placed her hands on her hips and looked around the dining hall. She didn't look like a sweet old lady any more.

'Norman!' she bawled. I jumped in my seat. 'Norrrrmmaannnn!'

An older man wearing a dusty jackeroo's hat and a pair of blue jeans with a silver belt buckle so huge you could cook a pizza on it, stepped out of the shadows and onto the stage. The young man with the tanned skin joined him. He looked down at me and winked.

Mrs Strickland cleared her throat.

'Waratah Grove is the foremost training facility in Australia for young equestrians. My name is Mrs Strickland and you will address me as such at all times. The two people standing behind me are my husband, Norman, and my grandson, Rex. You'll be seeing a lot of them during your stay at camp.'

'There is a god!' Spiral Curls whispered. She poked me in the ribs with one of those long pink nails. 'He's, like, so hot, eh?'

'So hot,' Juliette murmured.

I scrutinised Rex. He seemed to be quite a comfortable temperature to me.

'You will now be allocated your cabins,' Mrs Strickland continued. 'Each cabin is named after a champion Australian equestrian. Your first assignment will be to present a report on the namesake of your cabin.'

'Homework?' Spiral Curls yelped. 'Are you serious?'

Mrs Strickland landed a cold, narrow eye on Spiral Curls. 'Brooke Barnes, you know me well enough to know that I am always serious.'

So that was her name, Brooke. She was brave, that was for sure. If Mrs S had wanted me to do a ten-page assignment on horse poo I would have done it and asked her if she wanted an extra five pages on cow poo as well.

'Listen carefully for your name,' Mrs S continued. 'Your horses have already been assigned a stall number. You will find that your animal has already been installed in the appropriate stall.'

Animal? Honey? Not my Honey horse. Animals are creatures like dogs and cats and mice and lions. Horses are best friends.

Mrs S began reading aloud from a shiny black clipboard. I was assigned to Roycroft cabin with five other girls including Brooke and Juliette Salini. All the boys, from little kids with missing teeth to huge long things who looked like they could swallow a fridge whole, were assigned to Morgan. The last cabin, which was made up of the older girls, was called Hoy.

Brooke put her arms around my shoulders and squeezed me.

'We're together,' she said. 'Awesome!'

'Awesome,' Juliette said, nodding.

'We'll be, like, inseparable. The three of us. Best friends. How cool!'

'I'm so glad I met you guys,' I said. It was true. Waratah Grove would have been horrible without good friends and I already had two.

Brooke and Juliette flashed two of the most perfect smiles I'd ever seen.

'Want some?' Brooke offered me a piece of bubble gum. I popped it into my mouth, chewing happily with my new mates.

'Roycrofts!' called a voice. 'All Roycrofts this way, please.'

Brooke, Juliette and I, the Three Groveketeers, slid down the bench and took off together following the voice.

THREE
Roycroft Cabin

'Welcome home,' Kylie — the owner of the voice — said as she opened the door to Roycroft cabin. She was going to be our cabin 'mum' for the next four weeks.

'Wow,' I said at once. 'Wow, wow and wow.'

Brooke squeezed my arm, chomping on her gum, a wide grin spread across her face. 'Told ya. You'll love it here.'

I had to agree. The cabin was a big open room with six beds in a single row, separated by six small chests of drawers, a table and chairs and four comfy-looking armchairs. There was a shelf lined with books, two huge windows and a door that led to another, smaller room for Kylie. The walls were covered with portraits, photos and ribbons, just like in the dining room, and between the windows sat a huge trophy cabinet bursting with gold and silver cups, trophies and plates. The Roycrofts chattered over the top of each other, bags-ing beds.

'I guess I'd better let you claim your beds now and get it out of your systems!'

'Yes!' sang the Roycrofts, instantly leaping onto beds and opening and slamming drawers. I watched them, open-mouthed.

'Over here, Ashleigh!' Brooke waved to me frantically. She had one hand on the bed next to the wall and her foot on the bed beside her, reserving it for me. Juliette was already pretending to be asleep on the bed beside mine.

'Good thing I did all those ballet lessons,' Brooke said, rubbing her backside as I slid onto the bed.

'Comfy,' I said, testing the mattress for optimum springiness by bouncing up and down as high as I could. Who cares if I was now a sixth grader? Nothing beats bouncing on the bed.

Kylie clapped her hands twice and the chat died away. It was time for a 'getting to know you' session.

The Roycrofts sat down at the table and sized up each other for a moment. Brooke sat on my right, Juliette on my left. A tall pretty girl with large dark eyes sat opposite me. Her frizzy black hair was twisted into two bunches, like teddy bear ears, on top of her head. I smiled at her. She looked at me for a moment, then turned her head away. Maybe not everyone at the Grove was as friendly as Brooke and Juliette. I checked out the girl sitting beside her. She had deep dimples and very blue eyes. A wide-eyed little girl with two long braids sat at the end of the table.

Kylie kicked things off by telling us about herself. She turned out not just to be Kylie, but Kylie Henry, Pan Pacific Three-Day International Event Champion, three star! I had read about her in horse magazines and here I was sitting across the table from her. I was excited to learn we'd be seeing her for specialist cross-country instruction.

Brooke went next, telling the Roycrofts about her horse, Angel, a grey Anglo-Arab with whom she'd won the State Junior Dressage Championships the previous year.

I sucked in my breath. The silver mare was

Brooke's! Was she ever lucky. That mare was like moonlight on legs.

Next, Teddy Bear Ears introduced herself as Tash Symon. This was her third time at the Grove with her horse, Silverado. Dimples told us she was eleven-year-old Molly Bryant who owned a horse called Rebel. Juliette spent most of her turn staring at the ceiling and saying 'um'. Finally it was my turn.

My stomach squelched. I had one chance to make a good first impression. I pushed back my chair and stood up, licking my lips. They were dry. I didn't think I could choke out a single word.

'Hi,' I squeaked. Tash coughed loudly. 'Um, I'm Ashleigh Miller. You can call me Ash. Um, my horse is Honey, she's a chestnut, um.'

Brooke patted my back. 'Tell everyone how you won the Grove Junior Cross-Country Champs.'

'So you're Ashleigh Miller!' Molly sat up and leaned across the table towards me. 'I saw your ride. It was wonderful!'

My face burned. 'Th-thanks,' I stammered. 'Thanks a lot.'

I sat down quickly and covered my cheeks with my hands. I didn't usually feel so shy. But I was at

Waratah Grove and every girl sitting at the table was a champion. I really wanted them to like me.

'Thanks, Ash,' Kylie said warmly. She leaned forward and patted my arm. I felt a bit better.

Kylie turned to the little girl with the braids who hadn't said a word. I noticed at lunch she had a tooth missing at the front. 'Lena, would you like to say something?'

Lena shook her head and bit her bottom lip.

Kylie told us the little girl's name was Lena Jones. She was an eight-year-old who was away from home for the first time ever.

Lena dissolved into huge sobs. Her shoulders shook. Molly pulled a tissue out of her pocket and pressed it into Lena's hand. Kylie stood and took her other hand and tugged gently, leading her away from the table. 'I'll leave you guys to get to know each other for a while. Lena and I are going on a little walk. I'll be back later to take you on your official tour of the Grove. In the meantime you can unpack your things.'

Kylie left the room with a now distraught Lena in tow. Brooke and Tash sat silently at the table for a moment, checking each other out like lions trying to decide who to eat first.

'Good to see you again, Tash,' Brooke said at last. 'It's been, like, ages.'

Tash bristled. 'It's been, like, not long enough!' She pushed her chair back, stood up and left the room. Molly rushed after her.

Brooke grabbed my arm, her curls bouncing. 'You'd better stay away from her. For your own good.'

'Own good,' Juliette said, nodding.

'I'll keep it in mind,' I said, determined to stay as far away from Tash as possible. Brooke, Juliette and I started putting away our things, taping the pictures we'd brought from home to the wall space above our beds and talking about home. I missed home like crazy already and I missed Becky and Jenna, but it didn't hurt as much as I thought it would. I had two new friends and four amazing horse mad weeks to look forward to. And what could be better than that?

Kylie returned to take us on the tour she promised. One thing was certain — the Grove was like horse universe. I'd seen a small part of it during the Cross-Country Championships and I'd pored over the glossy brochure we'd been sent, but nothing prepared me for the reality. From our cabin, we trooped along after Kylie across the cobblestones to the dressage ring where there was a fully equipped sand dressage arena and stands. Kylie pointed to a huge shed-like building. It was the all-purpose undercover arena where lessons could continue in bad weather. Next, we were steered past the dressage ring to a showjumping ring with an impressive collection of colourful jumps and its own spectator grandstand. There was a warm-up ring, and just behind it, a large round yard for lunging. Kylie ordered us onwards and we came to the cross-country course (where I'd competed just a few months earlier) and bush trails. And that was just the start of it.

'Who's for a stable tour?' Kylie asked. The Roycrofts cheered.

Kylie marched us back in the direction we'd come and pointed to a large building that contained the offices, library and recreation room. Finally, the stables were ahead of us. I couldn't wait to be with Honey.

As we walked through the door, the first thing I noticed was the smell. A fresh and wonderful smell — a delicious mix of horses, hay, feed, tack, sawdust and wood. The door I was standing at was the halfway point of the stables. Stalls stretched to the left and right of me. The walls were so high, I wondered how anyone managed to open the windows that ran all along the top near the ceiling. The stalls looked roomy and each one had a nameplate and number on the door. Near the main door was a list of horses' names, their stall number and details of their feed requirements. There was an office to the right with a messy desk, three silver filing cabinets and a bookshelf.

'There's a map on the office wall,' Kylie announced above the 'oohs', 'ahhs' and 'wows'. 'So you can find your horse's stall. Have a look around and get a feel for the stables.'

The Roycrofts crowded around the map, then rushed off in all directions, as anxious to reunite with their horses as I was. I realised that I had found people who were just as horse mad as me. Just as I was about to make a dash for stall 13, I heard crying and looked around. It was Lena.

'What's wrong?' I asked.

Lena shook her head, tears pouring down her face.

I put my arm around Lena's shoulders. 'What is it? What's the matter?'

Lena hiccuped. 'I-I c-can't, remember w-where B-Biscuit is.'

I ran my finger across the map. 'Number five. That way.' I pointed right.

'Thanks, Ash-a-leigh.' Lena managed a watery smile and trotted to her stall. A cute brown pony was looking over the door and whinnied when she saw Lena.

Brooke was back from her visit already. She sighed loudly. 'Angel's in twenty-three. I *hate* that side.'

I studied the map. Stalls 1 to 17 ran in an anti-clockwise circle from the office. Stalls 18 to 27 ran behind. I was amazed. I had never seen such a huge stable.

Brooke smiled sweetly at me. 'Where's Haney?'

'Honey,' I said. 'Stall thirteen.'

'Rats, we're not next to each other.' Her face clouded over for a moment. 'Don't worry. You'd better go find Hinny. Kylie wants us to go up for dinner soon.'

'It's Hon —'

Brooke blew me a kiss and dashed away again.

I jogged down the aisle and spotted Honey at last. She had her head in a feed bin as usual. Her neighbour was a huge black horse, at least 17 hands, with four white socks.

'Here you are, gutsy,' I said, smiling to myself. I unlatched her door and let myself in, bolting it behind me. It was so good to see her! It had been hours. I hate being away from Honey. At home, I'm only ever away from her for school and sleep. I do my homework by my bedroom window so I can see her and sometimes I even eat my meals in her paddock.

I hugged Honey's neck and ran my hand over her withers and down her shoulder. Her muscles rippled beneath my hand. I felt like I was home at last. I realised then it didn't matter where I was. As long as I had Honey with me, home was where the horse was.

'Roycrofts!' I could hear Kylie calling from the door. 'Roycrofts, let's go!'

'Already?' I groaned. 'But I only just found you! Just a few more minutes, eh, Hon?'

I talked to her, telling her about what I'd been doing and rubbed the special place behind her ears that she liked so much. Her head drooped with pleasure.

'Ashleigh!'

I jumped.

'Ashleigh, hurry up.'

I peered over Honey's shoulder. Tash was glowering at me from the stall door.

'We've been waiting for you for ages.'

I gave Honey a last quick cuddle. She buried her face in the feed bin again and I jogged back down the aisle.

The Roycrofts trooped up to the dining room behind Kylie for the second time that day. Scrumptious smells were wafting from the open door. I'd forgotten I was starving! I could have eaten a barrel of chaff and molasses and begged for seconds.

There had been a few changes inside the dining room since lunch. Instead of the tables scattered around the room, there were only five long tables with benches. A helium balloon in the shape of a giant golden horseshoe floated above three of the tables, each with a ribbon tied to either end. Kylie pointed to the table with the ribbon that said 'Roycroft' then joined the other instructors on the long table that sat in front of the stage, Lena squeezed in beside her. Her eyes were still red and she had her finger in her mouth.

Brooke grabbed my hand.

'Let's sit here,' she said, plonking down on the bench right opposite Tash and Molly. Molly smiled but Tash refused to even look at us. Whatever her problem was I hoped she'd get over it. I didn't want to have my dream Waratah Grove stay ruined by a grouch.

My stomach growled like a hundred hooves beating against solid earth at once. I craned my neck for a look at the kitchen door. Why wasn't it opening?

My tummy ached. I could smell the delicious food, but it didn't seem to be coming out yet. There were forks, knives and serviettes laid out on the table but none of those made good eating.

'I'm starved,' I said.

Brooke leaned forward and shouted over the dining room chatter at the instructors' table. 'Kylie, Ashleigh's hungry. She says she wants to eat now.'

The dining room fell silent at once, then a few people laughed. Kylie frowned and gestured at us to be quiet. My face burned.

'Sorry!' Brooke said, squeezing my hand. 'I was only trying to help.'

I nodded. 'S'okay. It wasn't your fault.'

Brooke flicked a handful of curls over her shoulder. 'Are you sure? I mean, I don't want you to be, like, embarrassed.'

'I'm sure,' I said. 'It doesn't —'

The kitchen door flew open and Mr Strickland emerged pushing a huge food trolley. He was wearing a pink apron with yellow flowers on it and a tall white chef's hat. The Roycrofts giggled together.

'Our table first, our table first!' Tash groaned.

I smiled at her. She met my eyes then stared up hard at the ceiling.

The trolley stopped beside me and plates of juicy sausages, hot chips and crisp salad were passed along the table. I grabbed a fork and stabbed a sausage, took a huge bite and chewed. Mr Strickland placed a basket of buttered bread rolls and a bottle of tomato sauce in the centre of the table and wheeled the trolley away in the direction of the Morgans.

'Molly didn't get a plate!' I called out suddenly. The Roycrofts stared at the empty place in front of Molly.

Molly pressed her finger to her lips. 'Shh. It doesn't matter.' Her ears were red.

The kitchen door opened again. Rex Strickland, carrying a plate in one hand and a piece of paper in the other, stopped at our table. Juliette smoothed her hair and blinked at him.

'Molly Bryant?' Rex said, reading off the paper.

Molly raised her hand. 'That's me.'

'Dinner is served!' Rex said, putting a plate of salad, chips and mushroom risotto in front of her. She thanked him and he returned to the kitchen.

'Fair dinkum, he is so spunky, eh?' Brooke elbowed me in the ribs. I chewed on my sausage. 'I said he's spunky, eh, Ashleigh? Don't you reckon Rex is like, just so spunky, Ashleigh?'

I swallowed, nodding.

'Do you like him, Ash. Like, *like* him?'

Juliette crashed her knife and fork down hard on her plate. I could feel her blue eyes boring into my face. I had to change the subject.

'Molly, don't you like sausages?'

Molly shook her head. 'Uh-uh. I don't eat meat. I'm a vegetarian.'

Brooke nibbled on the end of a sausage. 'What for?'

'I love animals,' Molly shrugged. 'Why would I want to eat them?'

Brooke clucked her tongue. 'That's really interesting. Isn't it, Ash?'

I nodded, chunks of half-eaten sausage rolling around in my mouth.

Tash landed an eye on me for a moment, as though I was about to say something.

'Waratah Grovers!' Mrs Strickland was up on the stage. 'While you're eating we'll get on with some housekeeping.'

'Now the fun starts,' Brooke whispered, stabbing a chip with her fork.

'Waratah Grove is run like a tight ship and a tight ship never sinks!' Mrs Strickland declared as Mr Strickland appeared carrying an armful of stapled papers.

He handed one to every rider in the room. I gaped when I looked over mine. It was a timetable, listing all the classes, duties and activities we had to attend every day of the week. Even Sundays were strictly scheduled with leisure activities replacing lessons. Every rider had to be out of bed by six-thirty, be at breakfast by seven and be mucking out stalls by seven-thirty. Grooming was scheduled for eight, tacking up for eight-thirty and every rider had to be present in his or her class by nine o'clock sharp. There were two practical and two theory lessons per day plus stable and cabin duties. I was relieved to see there was a half-hour of free time squeezed into the afternoons and an hour of entertainment every night after dinner. Every minute of the rest of the day was planned right up until lights out at nine-thirty.

'They're being easy on us this year.' Tash shook her head, laughing.

'Whoa!' I gasped. 'This is unbelievable.'

'Now that you have examined your timetables I will introduce Waratah Grove's outstanding and very experienced instructors to you.' Mrs S indicated the instructors' table. As she introduced each one, they stood up and waved. Apart from Kylie, there was Alexander George from Morgan cabin, who had coached Australian national teams and would instruct us in dressage. Joanne Phillips, an Australian national champion, would be our showjumping instructor and the Hoy cabin 'mum'. Mrs S would be our Equitation instructor.

'I thought camp was supposed to be fun. This is worse than school,' Brooke moaned.

I sent her a sympathetic look — Waratah Grove was totally full on!

'Those of you who have been with us before will know all about graduation, but for those of you new to the Grove, open your ears.'

I poked around inside each ear. They were definitely open.

'Graduation,' Mrs S said again.

I gulped. Nobody had ever said anything about graduation before I came to Waratah Grove.

Mrs S pulled a pair of slim spectacles out of her shirt pocket and hooked them over her ears. She peered out over the top of them at the Grovers.

'You will receive twenty-four days of intensive instruction in three-day eventing and practical horse care and stable management.'

Eventing, wow! A year ago I was barrel racing at South Beach Stables, my old riding school in the city. And now here I was, about to learn eventing at Waratah Grove.

'At the end of that period you will be examined in each phase of the three-day event — dressage, cross-country and showjumping. You will have to pass each phase at C-grade level or above.'

I sucked in my breath. I had to pass dressage at C-grade level? I'd never tried dressage with Honey. I didn't know the first thing about it. Showjumping I thought I could maybe handle — after all, I'd jumped enough cross-country obstacles in the last few months to give me an idea of how to take on a post and rail jump. But dressage? I'd always been happy to leave dressage to Becky.

'Once you have completed your three-phase trials you will be examined in grooming and sit a theory exam,' Mrs S continued.

I couldn't believe what I was hearing. Had we driven right past the real Waratah Grove and landed in a military school instead?

'Only those riders who complete and pass each examination will be allowed to graduate from Waratah Grove. Those students will have their names inscribed on the Waratah Grove Honour Board, receive a certificate and trophy and leave the Grove infinitely better riders than when they arrived.'

I rubbed my forefingers on my temples, trying to take it all in.

'Finally,' Mrs S announced, 'those of you who have been with us before will recognise this.' She held up a large gold trophy.

'I want to win that so bad!' Tash sighed.

A boy from Morgan with sandy-coloured hair leaned over from his table. 'Don't we all!'

'The Waratah Grove Cup is up for grabs again,' Mrs S said. She placed the cup on the instructors' table. 'To all those new to the Grove, be aware that the Cup is rarely awarded, and when it is it goes to the rider who proves him or herself the most worthy equestrian. A rider who stands out from the crowd. Not necessarily a rider who always completes a perfect dressage test or never knocks a rail down in the jumping ring. There is no accumulation of points, no test. The winner will, in a way, choose themselves through their thoughts, words and deeds. I hope that amongst you sitting here tonight there is such a rider. Someone for whom riding horses is not just a sport, not just for fun; it is their life. It is ...' Mrs S fell silent for a moment, then cleared her throat. 'It is everything. The only thing.'

I knew what she meant. As I sat there on the hard wooden bench surrounded by the best of the best, I wished for only one thing — that the winner of the Waratah Grove Cup would be me.

FOUR

Ringmaster

I'd been up for hours, since way before the six-thirty bell. By the look of the Roycrofts I wasn't the only one.

After dinner we'd been sent off to entertainment, which was a choice between watching a movie or hanging around the library to read or use the computers. I'd sent a quick email home to Mum and Dad and started researching my assignment on the Roycroft family. There was a bell at nine for showers and we hit the hay by nine-thirty. It had been weird trying to snuggle into a strange bed in a room full of Roycrofts. I'd dropped off eventually, but had woken with a pounding heart while it was still dark. Today was my first dressage lesson and I'd never even tried it before. It was hard to believe that only yesterday morning I was sitting bareback on Honey in our paddock. It seemed an age ago.

I bolted for the dining room while Brooke was in front of the mirror struggling to tame her hair, promising her I'd save her the seat next to me. Breakfast was ready. It smelled wonderful. There was a buffet table arranged by the stage and I stared at the food, my mouth watering. Mr S, wearing his yellow-flower apron and chef's hat, handed me a plate piled with bacon, scrambled eggs, hash browns and toast. I helped myself to a glass of orange juice and settled down alone at the Roycroft table. The food was delicious.

Just as I was mopping up the last of my breakfast Brooke dashed into the dining room with Juliette. She was dressed in amazing riding clothes — spotless cream joddies, a white blouse, a cream vest and a neat blue jacket. Her wild curls were tied down and twisted into a bun at the base of her neck. For a moment she reminded me of someone.

Brooke saw me and waved. She slid onto the bench, beaming.

'Good brekkie?'

I nodded, swallowing. 'Yep. Sorry I didn't wait for you. I just want to get to the stables.'

Brooke shrugged. 'No probs. Just promise me we'll sit together at lunch.'

'Promise,' Juliette said.

'I promise.' I stood up and picked up my plate. There was a rubbish bin to scrape plates into and a bin for dirty dishes, glasses and cutlery.

Tash, Molly and Lena arrived, dressed in neat riding clothes.

'Hi, guys,' Molly said, waving.

'Are you wearing that for the lesson?' Tash said, raising her eyebrows and looking me up and down.

I looked down at my untucked dark blue Shady Creek Riding Club shirt, old beige joddies and scuffed riding boots. 'Yeah. I always wear this when I ride.' Well, hello to you, too, I thought.

'Ashleigh looks wonderful!' Brooke said. 'Don't scare her, Tash. We're, like, totally overdressed!'

Tash and Molly exchanged glances.

'Whatever you say, Brookey.' Tash nudged Molly and they headed towards the buffet table.

'Don't listen to her,' Brooke said as soon as they were out of earshot. 'I mean, Tash is weird. Have you seen what she does to that photo of hers? You know the one of that little kid?'

'Well, yeah.' I glanced at Tash.

Brooke's eyes were wide. 'She, like, kissed it goodnight! Can you believe it?'

'I, uh . . .' I took a step towards the door. 'Stables.'

Brooke blew me a kiss. 'No worries. See ya in the ring, Ash!'

'See ya!' I called after her. I wiped my mouth on a paper serviette, tossed it in the rubbish bin and was on my way to the stables before you could say dressage lesson.

'It's so good to see you, Honey. I feel like I've been away from you for days, months, years even!'

Mucking out had never been such fun.

'How about a groom?' I said, glancing at the clock on the stable wall. We were making good time. Most of the riders hadn't finished breakfast. I slipped a halter over Honey's ears and fastened it at the side of her face then clipped on a lead rope and tied her to the wall of the stall. She knew what was coming and seemed to be smiling. I rummaged in my grooming kit for a moment and pulled out my hoof pick, slipping it into my shirt pocket. I ran my hand down Honey's near side foreleg. She shifted her weight and raised her foot.

'Good girl,' I murmured.

I inspected Honey's foot, checking for stones and making sure her shoe was secure. I pressed her frog gently. She'd been in the float for hours the day before and even though she'd been wearing travel boots, I was worried about her feet and legs. Everything looked fine so I cleaned her hoof and set it down gently again.

Three more feet later and I was ready to give Honey a good comb with the dandy-brush. Her muscles rippled with pleasure as I ran the brush over her body, taking care not to knock the fine bones in her legs. I followed with the body brush and before long she was shining.

'You're looking good, Honey,' I said, puffing slightly. I love to groom her but it's hard work!

I ran the body brush gently over her face and forelock, then grabbed Honey's sponges from my grooming kit, dipping them, eye sponge first, into a bucket of water.

'Ashleigh, Ashleigh!'

'Hey!'

Brooke gave me a dazzling smile and leaned on the door of Honey's stall. Juliette hovered behind her, watching me.

'Watcha doing?' Brooke said as I sponged under Honey's tail.

I smiled. 'Exactly how much detail do you want me to go into?'

Brooke laughed loudly. 'Ashleigh, you are *sooo* funny!'

I closed my grooming kit and stretched my back. 'I'm going to get Honey's tack.'

'Got it.' Brooke indicated a saddle, saddle blanket and bridle placed carefully on Honey's stall. 'Ta-da!'

'Thanks!' I was gobsmacked. Brooke was turning out to be my best friend at the Grove. I imagined introducing her to Jenna and Becky. I'm sure they'd like Brooke as much as I did. 'But what about your tack?'

Brooke jerked her thumb towards Juliette. 'Jules got mine.'

I gave Honey's nose a quick stroke and settled her saddle blanket down just behind her withers. I noticed

Tash saddling her blue roan gelding, Silverado, in the opposite stall. She looked at Brooke and me with narrow eyes then turned her back to us.

'I've already organised a game of tennis for us at free time,' said Brooke.

I nodded, tightening Honey's girth. 'Sounds great! Now this place is sounding more like a resort.'

Brooke laughed loudly.

I slipped Honey's bridle over her ears and fastened it. She was all tacked up and ready to go. My tummy fizzed.

'This is so cool. I'm riding at the Grove!'

Brooke gave me her best smile. 'Good luck, buddy!'

'See you in the ring,' I said.

'With bells on.' With that, Brooke disappeared.

I pulled my helmet down over my head and led Honey out of the stall into the cobblestoned waiting area.

A gentle bell rang. It was nine o'clock and time for my very first lesson at Waratah Grove to begin. Alexander George, the dressage coach, strode into the waiting area wearing a dark green Waratah Grove polo shirt with 'Instructor' written across the

back in big white letters, black joddies, long black
boots and a broad-brimmed sunhat. His nose and
lips were smeared thickly with white zinc cream.

'Roycrofts!' he called. 'Roycrofts, you have two
minutes to be in the waiting area.'

In less than two minutes all six Roycrofts were
gathered with their horses. Five seconds later we were
following Alexander to the enormous warm-up ring.

'Line up mounted in a single row, riding club
inspection style, please,' he said.

I gathered my reins at Honey's withers, wedged
my left foot into the stirrup, and bounced into the
saddle. I gave Honey a gentle nudge, urging her
forward into the line. Brooke waved frantically.

'Over here, Ash! Over *here*!'

I pulled into line between Brooke and Juliette. We
grinned at each other.

'Good morning, Roycrofts, Alexander!' boomed a
voice. Mrs S strode into the warm-up ring, clipboard
in hand. Her hair was twisted into its usual tight roll.
She squinted up at us. 'I'll be doing inspection this
morning.'

She began with Lena, admonishing her for her
messy hair then moved on to Tash whom she praised

for everything except a scuff mark on the toe of her left riding boot. Molly survived with only an order to tidy Rebel's tail (there were straws of hay sticking out of it) and Juliette merely rolled her eyes when Mrs S made her remount Storm and correct her posture. I was next in line.

Mrs S stood in front of Honey. I sat as perfectly as I could in the saddle making sure my fingers were where they should be on the reins and that my heels were pointing slightly down at exactly the right angle. My shirt was now tucked in, I was wearing my brand-new helmet (thanks again, Santa) and Honey was sparkling like an equine disco ball in the morning sun. My back was straight, my chin was up — I was confident.

'Miss Miller, if you think that this is an appropriate way to present yourself for dressage you have got another think coming!'

I felt like I'd been smacked in the guts. What had I done wrong?

'Dismount at once!'

I shook my feet out of the stirrups and slid to the ground. My knees wobbled.

Mrs S sized me up for a moment, her eyebrows scrunched together and her lips thin as rice paper.

'Your boots are scuffed — it must be light years since they saw the inside of a tin of polish! Your shirt is fine for trail riding and cross-country but *totally* unacceptable for dressage. Your helmet has a mud stain on it and your jodhpurs look like they could walk themselves to the laundry!'

I stared at the ground, hoping an opening large enough for me to disappear into would materialise.

'Make sure it doesn't happen again! Remount!'

I mounted Honey, feeling the sting of hot tears in my eyes. I had never been so embarrassed in my life. Not even the time Honey threw me into a ditch right in front of Flea, King Creep of the Creek. Not even when Mum delivered my lunch to school, totally pregnant and wearing a pair of old blue plumbing overalls. My face burned. I could hear Molly and Tash muttering. It wasn't fair.

I glanced at Brooke. She met my eyes. Hers were wide. She shrugged and mouthed the word, 'Sorry.' She had, after all, said I was dressed fine. Maybe the rules had changed since her last visit.

'The way you present yourself says more about you than words ever can,' Mrs S announced. 'Many of you are here because you want to be champions. And some of you will be. You ride well. You have passion. But that is not enough. A champion is made from the inside. A champion understands that no detail is too small to be below their notice!'

Brooke passed inspection with flying colours and Mrs S marched away to inspect the Morgans who had already warmed up their horses and were now being put through their paces in the jumping ring.

'All right, let's get started,' Alexander said. 'And please call me Alex. I keep reminding Mrs Strickland, but ...'

The Roycrofts giggled together.

'We'll start with a warm-up. Begin at a walk, then move to a trot and on to a canter. You three in this corner, you three in the other — we don't want any accidents. Wide circles to start with then figures of eight.'

Alex made his way up to the stands where he sat watching us, every now and then scribbling in a folder.

I was grouped with Brooke and Juliette. Molly, Tash and Lena began warming up on the other side of the ring.

I tried to push Mrs S out of my mind and focus on Honey. That was all I ever needed to do. No matter what had happened to me or was happening around me, riding Honey, or even thinking about her, was enough to take me away into another world.

We walked in a few circles then, following Brooke's lead, I urged Honey into a rising trot. Juliette followed suit. Honey was a little stiff. A few more circles and I knew her muscles would be ready to canter. As we trotted around and around, I couldn't help but have a look at the other Roycrofts. Lena and Biscuit were cantering in figure eights already, looking as though they'd been born for each other. Molly and Rebel, her gorgeous black pony, were doing likewise. I could see Molly's lips moving and knew she was talking to him. She dropped her hand to his shoulder and patted him occasionally, praising him. Tash and Silverado followed, also at a canter. Tash looked straight ahead, totally focussed. Silverado's feet pounded on the soft surface of the warm-up ring in a perfect collected canter —

his neck was arched and his steps were light and springy, as though he was being powered by his hindquarters. They looked amazing together, like one being, just like Becky and her horse, Charlie. You don't see partnerships like theirs very often. I watched them for a while, spellbound, until Juliette's voice brought me back to reality.

'Ash-leigh!'

I realised Brooke had moved to a canter and I urged Honey to do likewise. Brooke was good. She looked good too and her horse, Angel, was stunning. Juliette bounced in the saddle, probably because she was craning for glimpses of the Morgans in the jumping ring.

We completed our set of figure eights and pulled up our horses. I was feeling better already, carefree and happy. Saddle-happy!

'Well done, girls!' Alex said, climbing down from the stands. 'Some lovely riding there. Now we'll cross to the dressage ring and see what you're made of, eh?'

Alex took the lead and we walked behind him single file. I'd never been inside a dressage ring before but had seen them heaps of times. The letters around the edges meant nothing to me. I wished I'd pumped Becky, Shady Creek's dressage queen, for information before I'd left. I wanted her with me now more than ever!

I had a good look around inside the ring. Apart from the arena itself there were stands for spectators, a shaded waiting area for horses and riders, a shaded judge's table and a wide margin around the arena where Alex stood, ready to give us our first lesson.

'First up, who has had dressage experience?'

Every Roycroft hand shot up except mine and Molly's. We smiled at each other, relieved.

Alex grinned. 'Good stuff! Has anyone here ever won a dressage competition?'

Tash and Brooke raised their hands.

'Even better!' Alex said. 'I'll be relying on you two to set the standard for everyone else.'

Brooke puffed out her chest with pride. Tash was casual; I couldn't tell what she was thinking.

Alex cleared his throat. 'So what do we need to know about dressage before we even set hoof in the arena?'

'Dressage is a French word which means "training",' Lena said at once. It was the first time I'd heard her speak without crying.

'Spot on, Lena,' Alex said, rubbing his hands together. 'What else?'

'It's hard!' Tash said, grinning.

'Spot on again,' Alex said. 'Anybody else?'

The Roycrofts stared at him, silent.

'Okay,' Alex began, scratching underneath his sunhat at his mop of dark hair. 'Every horse and every rider in any discipline can benefit from dressage training. In dressage we're trying to achieve a physically fit and obedient horse. Hands up anyone here who thinks that a fit and obedient horse is a good thing to have at, say, a riding club gymkhana.'

Six hands shot up without hesitation. Alex smiled.

'There we go. A horse that is flexible, responsive, balanced and well-schooled is a much better and more enjoyable ride than a horse who hasn't had any formal training since he, or she, was broken. Looks like a little dressage training could be useful to all of us.' Alex gestured towards the arena. 'What's that?'

'The arena, of course,' Brooke said.

'Tell us about it, Brooke.' Alex smiled warmly at Brooke.

'The arena is a rectangular shape,' Tash said before Brooke had time to open her mouth, '20 metres wide and 40 metres long at Preliminary and Novice levels, and marked out by boards and letters.'

'Excellent,' Alex said. Brooke's ears turned red and she shot Tash a poisonous look. 'What other amazing facts have you got hidden under your helmet, Miss Symon? What are the letters for?'

Tash casually swished at a fly with her hand. 'The letters are to show you where you should carry out a movement.'

'A champion in our midst!' Alex was in raptures. Molly applauded and Tash took a bow.

'We have a few basic facts and we have six wonderful horses and riders, so I think the next step is to observe you in action. I'd like to see you have a go at the most recent test you performed in competition. Molly and Ashleigh, just watch for now.'

Alex pushed his hat back a little with both hands, thinking. 'Tash, let's see what you can do.'

'No problemo.' Tash nodded at the Roycrofts and grabbed Molly's hand for a moment.

'Good luck, Tash!' Molly said.

Silverado entered the arena without any obvious command from his rider. He entered at the letter A and walked to the centre of the arena, halting at the X cone (the halfway mark) to salute the imaginary judges.

'Watching, you two?' Alex called.

'Yes,' I said. 'But what does this all mean? Why are those letters there? I don't get any of this yet.'

'Me neither,' Molly said.

'The arena is marked with a series of cones,' Alex began. I opened my ears. 'A is at the southern end and is the point of entry.'

Alex must have sensed my immediate confusion. 'That's where you enter the arena.'

I nodded. 'Oh.'

'On the right side we have the letters F, B and M, all spaced 14 metres apart, with 6 metres between the ends of the arena and the first letters. On the left are K, E and H.' Alex pointed to the cones as he spoke. Tash continued at a walk before springing into a perfectly smooth canter.

'In the middle are D, X and G. X is the centre of the arena. You must stop there at the start of the test and salute the judge, who, if they were here today, would be sitting behind the northern wall, behind the C cone.'

'X,' Molly muttered. 'Salute the judges. Got it.'

'Look closely,' Alex said. 'K, D and F line up. So do E, X and B and so on. Now concentrate on Tash and Silverado. I'll talk you through what they're doing.'

Tash and Silverado were just amazing together. I watched them, awestruck, my mouth hanging open. By the time they were finished I ached to be as good a rider as Tash, to be able to make it look as easy as she did. I hadn't notice a single command from her and yet Silverado mastered movements that Alex had called out, such as pirouettes and travers, without a hiccup.

'Well done!' Alex shouted over the applause.

Tash returned to the group with the same casual look she had before. It was all in a day's work.

'Who'd like to go next?'

Lena's hand shot up. 'Me!'

'Okay, Lena, give it all you've got!'

Lena and Biscuit, her cute brown pony, entered the arena in the same way Tash had with Silverado. She performed a perfect, but much shorter, test.

Alex was impressed. 'Fantastic! Brilliant! Wonderful!'

Lena giggled with delight.

'That was unbelievable!' I gushed.

'Yeah, it's, like, unbelievable that such a little kid can do dressage,' Brooke said suddenly. 'I totally agree with you, Ashleigh.'

Lena's face fell. She bit her bottom lip and looked to Tash for reassurance. Tash looked at me. There was anger in her eyes.

'That's n-not what I meant,' I stammered, confused. 'I meant that Lena was so amazing out there.'

Brooke gave me a sweet smile. 'Of course she was. Nobody here would deny that.'

'But —' I began. I scratched my helmet, confused. What had just happened?

'Ashleigh Miller,' Alex said. 'Want to have a go?'

'I've never done any dressage!' I said.

Tash coughed. 'So who are you to criticise?'

'But I wasn't —'

'It's okay,' Alex said. 'I'll tell you what to do.'

I looked to Brooke for help. She waved at me, beaming.

'Just have a go, Ash,' Brooke chirped. 'It's not as hard as it looks.'

That didn't exactly instil any confidence in me. It hadn't looked hard to me at all. Tash and Lena had made it look dead easy. So if it looked hard to Brooke, how hard was it really?

I gathered my reins and nudged Honey gently, trying to be as subtle as Tash. Honey took a few steps towards the arena then stopped, tossing her head again and again.

I stroked her neck, making soothing noises. This wasn't like her. Thinking she may just have been a bit spooked I urged her on. She took another few steps and stopped dead, biting down hard on the bit and shaking her head. I nudged her again and she went into reverse, backing straight into Storm. Juliette let out a loud scream.

'Control your horse!' Alex shouted.

I gathered up my reins and pulled Honey's head in then applied more pressure to her sides. She lurched forward like a startled frog in a series of wild leaps and crashed into the arena at K, finally stopping when Alex grabbed her reins.

'What's going on?' he said, stroking Honey's neck. She was breathing hard, eyes rolling.

I dismounted; my legs were shaking and my heart was pounding. 'I don't know. I have no idea. She only spooks at plastic bags.'

Alex tightened his grip on her reins, moving his hand up under her chin. He looked around the dressage ring. 'There aren't any in here. Too many oats, perhaps. Up you get.'

I remounted and patted Honey's neck.

'Try a quiet walk to settle her. Then we'll start again.'

Alex left the arena. I peered at the nearest letter. We were at F.

'Walk to X,' Alex called. 'Now salute the judge.'

'How?'

Some of the Roycrofts giggled. Brooke gave me the thumbs up and Molly waved cheerfully. Tash was watching with cold eyes, her face blank.

'Take your right hand from the off rein,' Alex called. I obeyed. 'Good. Now hold both reins in your left hand and hold your right hand just behind your knee. That's it!'

I was stoked. I was actually doing real dressage for

the first time. The dream was there before I'd even collected my reins again. I'm representing Australia. The eyes of the horsy world are on me and Honey. We win and the gold medal is placed around my neck. I look down at it, pick it up and kiss it before holding it up high in victory. The crowd applauds. The Australian flag is raised high above my head. I sing the anthem and . . .

'Ashleigh, are you with us?'

'What?' I blinked at the Roycrofts who were giggling like mad. 'Sorry, I'm ready.'

'Walk her from X to A,' Alex called, scribbling in his folder.

I nudged Honey's sides and she moved forward, past the D. Honey was doing well, walking calmly and smoothly. Her head bounced up and down, her mane swished and her ears were pricked forward. She was attentive and alert — perfect. This is easy! I thought.

'When you reach A, I'd like you to turn left and trot from A to F, then F to M,' Alex said. The Roycrofts sat mounted behind him, watching me.

Following my signal Honey began to trot. Her hooves moved rhythmically, tossing up the sand on the arena floor. The saddle rocked gently beneath me. This is what it was all about. This and only this. To ride; it was all I needed. To breathe and to ride. We approached B. I grinned to myself, sure that by graduation day we would have mastered the basics. I could go home and surprise Becky, maybe even compete with her some day.

Suddenly, as we passed B, I felt Honey tense. I had no time to react before she reared, lashing out with her forelegs. I panicked for a moment, trying to remember all my training, and grabbed fistfuls of her mane. I shook my stirrups free, ready to jump.

'Don't pull the reins!' Alex called, leaping into the arena.

Honey touched down and went into reverse again, nearly knocking him down.

I gathered and shortened my reins. 'Whoa!' I cried, trying to turn her. 'Honey, stop!'

I fought for my stirrups but it was too late. Honey shied violently and I hit the sand. Alex dived for the reins but Honey spun around then galloped out of the dressage ring.

'I'll get her!' Tash yelled, gathering her reins and taking off after Honey.

Alex knelt beside me where I lay, winded, on the sand. 'You okay?'

I nodded and tried to sit up.

'Lay still for a while,' he said, examining my face. 'Get your breath back.'

'I've got her!'

I sat up immediately. Tash was leading Honey back into the dressage arena. I got to my feet and dusted myself off, embarrassed. Tash's ride had been awesome. Mine — awful! Tash handed me my reins and I thanked her. I checked Honey's legs for injuries and pulled the reins over her head, then sprang back into the saddle.

'Where were we up to?' I asked Alex.

'What are you doing?' he said, frowning.

'I'm finishing the test.' I gathered my reins, sending telepathic pleas to Alex. I had to leave the arena on horseback. I had to prove to him and the Roycrofts that I wasn't scared.

Alex grimaced. His dark eyes were serious. 'You don't have to do this.'

'I do.' I gathered my reins and urged Honey back to B, the point where everything had gone so wrong.

'Ask her to trot,' Alex called. 'Squeeze her middle.'

Honey felt my command to trot.

'Good. Now keep your hands firm on the reins. Keep your outside leg on her and she'll keep up the pace. That's good!'

We trotted down the right-hand side of the arena past the M cone and turned left at the northern wall in the direction of the C cone. I turned Honey left in the very middle of the northern wall at C and continued to trot down the centre line of the arena on to X where she stopped perfectly still.

'Well done, Ashleigh!' Alex called. The grimace was replaced by a warm smile. 'Well done.'

Honey walked calmly from the arena and I worked hard to keep my face from cracking as I pulled her up in line next to Brooke who leaned over and patted my knee. 'Never mind!' she said. 'It's only your first time. Mind you, nothing like that has ever happened to me, like, never! But you'll get better.'

'Thanks,' I muttered, fixing my gaze on Juliette who was taking her turn in the arena.

'Hey, I have a great idea!' Brooke gasped. 'What if you, like, get rid of that horse — mares are so high strung. Get yourself a gelding instead.'

My eyes narrowed and I clenched my teeth, ordering my mouth to behave. 'You have a mare, Brooke.'

Brooke laughed, her white teeth flashing in the sunlight. 'But I can *handle* her. Not everyone can handle a mare. You and Hinny obviously aren't suited.'

'Her name's Honey and she suits me fine,' I said, fighting back tears.

'I was only trying to help,' Brooke said, her green eyes looking wounded. She turned her attention to Juliette who'd finished her test.

Molly had a try next and with Alex instructing, Rebel turned in a perfect first-time performance. It wasn't fair. I had dreamed about Waratah Grove for months and now that I was actually here I stank! I decided I would see Mrs S and tell her myself. I was quitting the Grove and nobody was going to talk me out of it.

FIVE

Friends

So that was the beginning of my spectacular dressage career and the end of my first lesson at the Grove. I didn't quit. I cooled Honey out in the warm-up ring, gave her a quick groom in her stall and turned her out into the day paddock behind the stables where the horses spent a few hours relaxing while their riders did theory lessons, stable duties or had lunch. While Honey was grazing and making new friends (she especially seemed to like Molly's horse, Rebel) I tidied her stall, filled her water trough and cleaned her feed bin. I would have been happy to hide in the stables all day if it hadn't been for the hideous growling-like-a-Tassie Devil noises coming from my stomach.

The lunch bell rang as I was digging around for saddle soap in my grooming box and my aching tummy ordered me to abandon all thoughts of cleaning my tack, even though it would have given me a really good excuse to avoid everybody.

I scrubbed my hands at the sink and slunk out of the stables, catching a glimpse of Honey who didn't appear even slightly ashamed of herself.

I slipped into the dining hall hoping no one would notice me. After serving myself a huge slab of lasagne and salad I sat at the Roycroft table, which was almost ready to collapse under the weight of ice-cold jugs of orange juice, water, green cordial, baskets of crunchy bread rolls and bowls of fresh fruit.

As I sat down an older girl at the Hoy table gave me a smile but none of the three Roycrofts at the table even looked up. The Morgan boys were devouring their lunches and talking about seconds. Molly and Tash stared at their plates and Lena made off for the scraps bin before heading back to the stables.

I had barely swallowed the first bite when two immaculate riding outfits landed on the bench, one on either side of me.

'We've been looking for you everywhere,' Brooke said. 'We were so worried about you.'

'So worried,' said Juliette, nodding gravely.

I poked at my lasagne with my fork, feeling tears well up in my eyes. I thought about home, how Mum would be sitting at our table in our kitchen eating lunch all alone. Dad would be at work at the hospital. Honey's paddock would be empty and Becky would be grooming Charlie. A wave of homesickness washed over me and the first tears spilled down my face, landing in my salad.

'Your horse, um, Handy, needs some serious schooling, Ashleigh. I feel so sorry for you! It must be so awful to have a horse with behaviour problems. Ashleigh? What's wrong?'

I wiped my nose with the back of my hand. 'Nothing.'

Brooke leaned in so close to me I could make out a tiny scar above her eyebrow. 'You're crying! Juliette, Ashleigh's crying! What's wrong, Ashleigh? Why are you crying?'

'I'm not,' I croaked. It was hard to get the words out with that yucky tight feeling in my chest and the enormous sticky lump in my throat. 'It's my allergies. Hay fever. I get it all the time.'

'But you've been fine up till now. If you're feeling sick I'll take you to sick bay. You'll, like, miss this afternoon's lesson, but no one will mind.'

I managed a smile. 'I'm okay, don't worry about it.'

Brooke slipped her arm around my shoulder, concern etched on her face. 'Are you sure?'

I nodded.

Brooke patted my back and blew me a kiss. 'See you in a tick!'

She made a beeline for the buffet, Juliette hard on her heels, waving at the table of hungry Morgan boys as she passed them. I gobbled my lunch and made a dash to the scraps bin, then the plate bin and finally the door. I felt mean to leave without telling Brooke. But I had to get back to Honey. It was free time and although I should have been playing tennis with Brooke, all I wanted was to be with my Honey horse.

Honey was grazing happily. I called out to her and she trotted over to the fence. I held out my hand to stroke her nose and she nuzzled at my fingers for a treat.

'I haven't got anything, Honey. We're not in Shady Creek. I can't just raid the fridge.'

Honey dropped her nose to the ground and tore at a patch of lush grass.

'Why did you do that in the arena?' I said, running my hand down her mane. She snorted and shook her head. 'What was that all about?'

Honey lifted her head and rubbed her face against my shoulder, trying my hands a second time as though an apple might appear by magic.

'I told you I don't have anything! I'll try and sneak you a treat from the fruit bowl after dinner.'

'Here,' said a soft voice behind me. 'Does she like carrots?'

I spun around. Molly was leaning on the gate, watching me, her hand outstretched and holding a fat carrot.

'Where'd you get that?'

Molly grinned. 'There are some advantages to being a vegetarian, you know.'

I laughed, feeling much better, and fed Honey the carrot. Once she was sure there were no more treats, she headed for a patch of green grass, leaving Molly and me alone.

I turned to her and held out my hand. Molly clasped it and grinned. 'Friends?'

'Friends,' I said, relief washing over me like cool water.

We found a tree to sit under and chatted for a while, watching the horses. Molly told me about her pets. She showed me a picture of her three dogs, another of her two cats and yet another of her chooks. I asked to see one of her family but she hadn't remembered to bring any with her.

'What brings you to the Grove?' I asked.

'Early birthday present. I promised Mum and Dad I wouldn't ask for anything else.' Molly tugged on a long piece of grass. 'They said this stay was good for at least the next six birthdays, but I'll talk 'em round.'

'How do you know Tash?' I was dying to find out why she was so cool to Brooke and me.

'I met her yesterday. When we arrived. She's nice.'

'Yeah.' She'd caught Honey for me but other than that I couldn't see anything nice about her at all.

'Did you know she's State Under-13s Dressage Champion?'

I shook my head. How could I have known that? Tash had barely looked at me let alone talked to me.

All I knew about Tash was that she had a little sister whose photo she'd taped to the wall above her bed. I'd actually seen her saying goodnight to the photo, which I thought was a bit weird. But hey, I talk to Honey all the time and she's never answered me, not once.

'And you? Brooke and Juliette?'

'Same as you — met them yesterday. They seem really sweet.'

'Hmm.' Molly smiled briefly then looked away.

A bell rang and Molly looked at her watch. 'Oodles of noodles! It's one o'clock!'

We scrambled to our feet and jogged to the stables. It was time for our practical stable management lesson with Mrs S and being late was not an option!

SIX

Jump to It

The Roycrofts filed into the jumping ring at nine o'clock sharp the next morning for our first lesson with Joanne, the jumping coach. Our horses were warmed up and limber and we were itching to get started.

I'd seen the ring from the outside and thought it was amazing, but from the inside it was amazing to the power of 500 (who says I never listen in Maths?)! There was a full-sized showjumping course of fences, twelve in all. Some were oxers, which were jumps made from long white poles with red, blue or yellow stripes, propped up by a white wing at each end. Some were double oxers, which were the same as oxers except there were two bars. There was even a jump that had been made to look like a low red-brick wall with two red and white striped poles on top. That wasn't all. Joanne had laid out some blue and white trotting poles and set up a course of basic raised poles and cavaletti — low jumps made from a single pole fixed to two 'X' shapes. Cavaletti are great because you can easily change their height just by turning them over.

The fences were new, clean and left the old Shady Creek Riding Club jumps for dead. Gary Cho, my Riding Club instructor, had built most of our club's jumps himself out of scraps of wood, unwanted drums and bits of old doors, but these were real, professional show jumps. I sized them up and shivered. I'd jumped cavaletti lots of times, but the fences! I'd never jumped anything like them, not even at my old city riding school, which was much fancier than Shady Creek Riding Club.

Joanne had us line up for inspection. Either she was much softer than Mrs S or I'd done everything right because I passed inspection without a hitch. Brooke was told to go and wash the clown paint from her face. I sent her a sympathetic look.

'She could try washing out her mouth while she's at it,' Tash mumbled.

'Can any of you tell me why you're here?' Joanne asked.

I looked at the Roycrofts. Nobody wanted to be the first to say anything.

'To learn how to jump?' I asked.

'Yes, what else?'

'What else would we be doing in a jumping ring?' Tash said. Molly giggled.

Joanne smiled. 'You're here to learn eventing. Hasn't anyone read their timetable?'

The Roycrofts nodded in unison. Brooke scowled at Joanne instead, her newly washed face pale without its thick coating of make-up.

'Has any one of you noticed that you're learning dressage, jumping and cross-country? Anyone realise that these are the three phases of eventing?'

We nodded again.

Joanne had us dismount, tie our horses to the fence and walk the jumping ring.

'Get up close and personal with every jump,' she said. 'You need to know them inside out and back to front.'

'How about upside down?' Tash said, her face crinkled up into a huge grin.

Joanne smiled. 'Let's hope not.'

Brooke and I paired up and scrutinised the first jump, a double oxer painted red and white.

'Looks like a giant candy cane,' Brooke said. 'Like, yum!'

'Looks big.' I'd never jumped anything like it and it was the first jump of the course. 'They'll probably get worse.'

Brooke and I linked arms. Juliette watched us from the parallel spread fence she was supposed to be inspecting with her partner, Lena. Molly and Tash were giggling together by the straight fence, a neat fence with three yellow and white poles, the first of which was at least a metre high supported by what looked like a mini white picket fence and shrubs on each side. Brooke watched them for a moment then pulled me close, grinning.

'Are you thinking what I'm thinking?'

I shrugged. 'I dunno. What are you thinking?'

Brooke charged towards the parallel, dragging me along with her. Tash and Molly stopped talking at once. She gave them a tight little nod, then tapped the fence. She let go of my arm and walked around the fence, shaking it here and there and measuring it against her own height. Tash, Molly and I watched her, waiting to see what she would do next.

'Too easy,' she said finally. 'I've jumped heaps higher than this. I'm a B-grade jumper. This is for babies. I thought Grove was meant to, like, challenge us.'

Tash groaned and shook her head. I looked over my shoulder, hoping Joanne hadn't heard.

'These jumps are too easy,' Brooke said.

Tash folded her arms and fixed her eyes on Brooke's face. 'Is that right?'

Brooke took a step towards Tash. 'Yeah, that's right. And Ash agrees with me. Don't you, Ash?'

Three pairs of eyes bored into my face. I gulped and held up my hands, surrender-style.

'Um, um,' I stammered.

Brooke went on. 'Ash and me are friends and friends stick together, don't they, Ash?'

'Yeah.' I nodded, but I was trembling all the way to the tips of my riding boots.

'If that's the case we'll get Joanne to fix 'em higher, just for you.' Tash glared at me.

'No, um ... they're fine. Th-thanks.'

'Back to your horses!' Joanne called. The horse gods had come to my rescue.

Tash pushed past me. Molly followed, but gave me a smile. Brooke squeezed my hand. 'Do you see what she's like? Tash doesn't get along with *anybody*.'

I sighed, exasperated. 'I just want us all to be friends.'

Brooke put her arm around my shoulders and propelled me back towards the horses. Lena, Tash, Molly and Juliette were already mounted. 'Time to wake up Cinderella, 'cause it, like, ain't gonna happen.'

I didn't want to believe it, but the look on Tash's face was pretty convincing. She could have frozen the ring with just her eyes. I'd never seen anyone look so mad. Not even my parents that time when I'd found a horse to buy online and he was delivered bright and early the next day in our driveway. An ugly memory. A very ugly memory indeed.

Once I was in the saddle I felt better. Joanne launched us headfirst into our first lesson.

'We're going to start on some polework. It'll be a good opportunity to assess your riding and where you're at, jumping-wise.'

'Boring,' Brooke said, yawning hugely.

'Thanks for the input. The poles have been placed just under one and a half metres apart, which is perfect for the size of all your horses. Biscuit is our smallest pony on 12.2 hands. But this distance should suit her just as well as Angel, who comes in at 14 hands.'

Brooke shot up her hand. 'Joanne, that's not fair. I was doing poles, like, years and years ago. I want to jump.'

Joanne smiled. 'It won't kill you. Anyway, it's a great warm-up for the real stuff. Let's go. Ashleigh, you first.'

I counted the poles. Six in all, painted in blue and white stripes.

'Start her at a walk,' Joanne said. 'Make sure you ride in a straight line right in the middle of the poles. Don't rush. When you're comfortable, try a rising trot.'

I walked Honey a few times over the poles. It was foal's play for her. Sensing she was bored I squeezed my legs. She moved into a trot. I circled her and we rode over them again.

'Perfect. Go to the raised poles. Molly, your turn.'

I pulled Honey towards the raised poles, which had white blocks under alternate ends, while Molly took Rebel over the first course. Rebel took them in his stride and before long Molly was riding over the raised poles with Honey and me.

Lena, Tash and Juliette cleared the course, leaving Brooke and Angel.

'Okay, Brooke, go for it,' Joanne said.

Brooke shook her head. 'No way.'

'Brooke, take the poles.'

Brooke sneered. 'My parents are paying for me to jump real fences. They didn't send me to pony preschool.'

Joanne flushed. 'You're on a warning, Brooke,' she replied. Her ears were pink. 'One more comment and you're out of the lesson.'

Brooke rolled her eyes and sighed. She kicked Angel hard and she leapt to an uneven trot.

'Keep your hands still,' Joanne yelled. 'Balance in the saddle.'

Angel struck a pole with a loud thud. Tash whistled. 'What a champion.'

'It's not her fault,' Molly said under her breath.

'Did you see the way Brooke kicked her? She almost scared the saddle off her.'

Brooke rode over the course until Joanne was satisfied and moved her to the raised poles.

'Good,' she said finally. 'Now we try the cavaletti.'

'Hallelujah!' Tash cried.

'There are five stages in a jump, guys,' Joanne said, perching herself on the fence. 'Who knows what they are?'

'Approach,' said Tash.

'Take-off.' Molly grinned.

'Suspension, landing and get-away,' I said quickly.

Molly and I beamed at each other.

'Great!' Joanne said. 'These cavaletti are simple, but they're the best way to build your confidence and skills as you learn how to jump. We'll start with one cavaletto then move to pairs of cavaletti, threes and then as many as six. Who'd like to be my guinea pig?'

'Me,' Brooke said. 'Don't forget I'm a B-grade jumper.'

'With an A-grade mouth,' Tash said.

I gave Tash a look. Molly stifled giggles.

'Okay,' Joanne said. 'Take your stirrups up two notches. And when you're jumping, keep your hands low.'

'I know, I know.' Brooke moved Angel into position.

'As you approach the jump, lean forward. Just maintain a light contact with Angel's mouth. Understand?'

Brooke nodded. 'Of course I do.'

'Do one lap of the ring at a canter and take the cavaletti.'

Brooke urged Angel into a canter around the ring and approached the jump. I watched her carefully, waiting for her to lean forward. She sat stiffly in the saddle.

'Lean forward!' Joanne yelled. 'Hands up.'

Brooke obeyed, but it was too late. Angel cat-jumped the cavaletto. Brooke slipped in the saddle and yanked hard on her reins, jabbing Angel in the mouth. Angel tossed her head and skidded to a halt.

'Let's hear it for the B-grade jumper!' Tash slow-clapped.

Brooke flushed, gritting her teeth. The memory of my dressage disaster was fresh. Messing up at the

Grove was embarrassing enough without Tash's loud observations. Not everyone was perfect at everything.

'Leave her alone, Tash,' I snapped. 'It's our first lesson.'

Tash gave me a look that made my chest squeeze. 'Why don't you go next, Ashleigh?'

Brooke pulled up beside me. 'That's such a cool idea. I'd love to see you and Homey jump.'

'It's Honey!' I couldn't believe that Brooke, who was supposed to be my best Groveketeer buddy, couldn't remember my horse's name.

Brooke sat mounted on Angel. The gorgeous silver mare stood perfectly still, her dark gentle eyes watching, her silky ears flicking this way and that.

'Ready to go then, Ashleigh?' Joanne asked.

I nodded. 'Yes.'

'Okay, then. You're pretty familiar with cross-country jumping so I'm happy to let you have a go. Just make sure you keep your seat in the saddle as you approach and your knees and lower legs close to Honey's sides.'

'Okay,' I said. My heart started to thump.

'As you feel her take off, let your hands and arms follow forwards.'

'Got it.' I moved Honey into the starting position.

'We'll show 'em,' I whispered to Honey. Her ears pricked up. I patted her neck, feeling her warmth seep into my palm and sized up the course. There were six cavaletti spaced about 3 metres apart. They looked about half a metre tall.

I nudged Honey into a canter and rode once around the ring. We approached the first jump. My heart was beating hard. I leaned forward just as Honey took off, looking straight ahead through her ears. My back was straight. I moved my hands and shoulders forward and sank my weight into the stirrups. Honey tucked in her front legs and stretched out her neck. We sailed over the jump and landed, all in a heartbeat. My worries melted away. I took up the reins again and prepared for the second jump. Honey took one stride and sailed over. Then the third, fourth and fifth jumps.

We approached the last jump. I concentrated on Honey, on the beat of her steps and the sound of her mane swishing as she cantered. Honey took off. I felt her body tense as she sprang from her hindquarters. My heart sang with sheer exhilaration. She cleared the jump.

SEVEN
The Whinny of Change

'What's going on?' I grumbled, sitting bolt upright in bed. I looked at the clock on the wall. It was a quarter past six in the morning.

I blinked, rubbing at my eyes. I was confused. Tash was kneeling on the floor crying hysterically, Molly had her arms around Tash's shoulders and Lena was picking up what looked like dozens and dozens of tiny pieces of paper, no bigger than Smarties, from the floor beside Tash's bed.

'W-who would do s-such a thing?' Tash sobbed. 'It's s-so mean. It's just so m-mean!'

'What happened?' I insisted. I got out of bed and crouched down next to Tash.

'Her photo,' Molly said grimly. 'You know, that one of her sister? Someone's snipped it up.'

'Into a gazillion pieces,' Lena said, showing me a handful of fragments.

'Wow,' I said. I couldn't believe it. That photo must have meant a lot to Tash. More than I ever realised. We weren't exactly close, but I hated to see her like this. 'Where's Kylie?'

'Stables,' Molly said. 'I heard her leave.'

Tash shook her head, crying so hard now that she couldn't speak. Her nose was running but she didn't care.

I left Tash and scrambled over my bed, shaking Brooke. She yawned, then smiled up at me sleepily.

'What's happening?' Brooke groaned, then let out a huge yawn.

I told her about the photo. She raised her eyebrows and yawned again. 'Really? Sorry, Ash. I'm just so tired.'

Juliette sat up in bed. Her white hair was sticking up in all directions and her eyes seemed to be stuck together.

Tash wiped her face with her hands and cleared

her throat. 'It-it couldn't have been any of you. Y-you all know how much Emma means to me.'

'Maybe one of the Morgans. A couple of them are prize idiots,' Molly said.

'Hey!' said Juliette defensively. I gaped at her. It wasn't often she said anything without Brooke having spoken first.

'Why don't we ask around?' Brooke said. 'Come with me, Ash.'

Tash sniffled. 'Why are you suddenly being Miss Nice?'

'Tash, we're horse people. We have to help each other out, even if we have our differences.' Brooke threw back her covers and stuffed her feet into her slippers. 'Ready, Ash?'

I jammed on my slippers and, still in my brand-new, bought-for-camp pyjamas, waited by the door for Brooke, who was stretching luxuriously.

'Ash, get your robe on. It's probably freezing out there.' Brooke pulled her own robe on and tied the belt tight around her middle.

I smiled at her. We hadn't known each other long, but she looked out for me. I grabbed my robe from the foot of my bed and hauled it on. A small, square piece of paper, no bigger than a Smartie, drifted from the robe and landed at my feet.

Tash wiped her face with her hand, frowning. 'What's that?'

I stared at the paper, frozen to the spot.

Tash crouched at my feet. She picked up the paper and stared at it. She looked horrified. Like she was holding something poisonous. 'What's this?' she repeated.

I shrugged, jamming my hands into the pockets of my robe. I could feel something in my pockets. I pulled out my hands. More of the tiny pieces of paper came out with them, drifting to the floor like snowflakes.

Tash watched them, then looked up at me. I'd never seen anyone look so ... *shocked*. 'You!'

I felt like I'd been hit in the guts by a hay bale. 'I didn't do it!'

'What do you mean you didn't do it?' Tash shrieked.

'I-I didn't. Really.' I met the Roycrofts' eyes, appealing for help. They watched me silently.

'How could you?' Tash cried.

'Brooke, tell them,' I pleaded. I felt like a mouse backed into a corner by a tribe of ravenous cats.

Brooke stepped forward. 'Your pockets are full of photo paper, Ashleigh.'

I wanted to scream, but I gritted my teeth instead and spoke very slowly to make sure every one of the Roycrofts understood. 'I didn't do it. I'd never do anything like that.'

'You *were* pretty mad at Tash in yesterday's lesson, though,' Brooke said, biting her bottom lip. 'And you've never really liked her.'

Tash threw up her hands. 'Now it all comes out!'

I shook my head. 'It's not true. I swear!'

'It's not true about the photo part or the "you've-never-liked-me" part?'

My chest swelled with fury. 'Well, you've never exactly been best friend material yourself, Tash.'

'Have you ever wondered why?'

The Roycrofts looked from one of us to the other as though they were watching a tennis match.

'I'm getting Kylie,' Molly said. She dashed from the cabin in her pyjamas, slamming the door behind her.

'Don't fight!' Lena cried. 'Tasha, I'm scared.'

Lena ran into Tash's waiting arms. Tash held her close and stroked her hair.

'Don't worry,' she said soothingly. Brooke and Juliette stood behind them, glaring at me and shaking their heads in disgust. I was so confused. Why hadn't Brooke backed me up? Right from the first day we'd been friends. And now when I needed her most she'd chucked me.

'Brooke,' I said. 'What's happening?'

Brooke's eyes narrowed. 'I'm sorry, Ashleigh. I don't think we can be friends any more.'

'Not friends,' Juliette said.

In my whole life I had never felt so alone. It was like somewhere, somehow, every happy thought or feeling I'd ever had or would ever have had galloped away like a herd of brumbies, never to return.

The door swung open and Kylie burst into the cabin with Molly.

'Roycrofts, get dressed. You should be at breakfast now.' Kylie took in the situation. 'Then get yourselves to the stables quick smart. We have our first cross-country lesson today and I accept no excuses for tardiness.'

The Roycrofts sprang into action. I stood there, stunned.

'Ashleigh, before you go to breakfast I'd like a word,' Kylie said. 'A-about Honey. Yes, Honey.'

The Roycrofts dressed in cold silence and filed out of the cabin one by one. I hung back. Kylie closed the door after Brooke (who seemed to be very interested to find out what Kylie needed to tell me about Honey) and asked me what had happened.

I sat down on my bed and buried my face in my hands. There was no one around I needed to keep myself together for. In between sobs I told her the story. It was painful to say it out loud, but in a way I wanted to hear it. I had to know that everything that had happened was real. Kylie let me finish and when I had cried my last great heaving sob, she told me to wash my face, go to breakfast and get myself to the cross-country course.

'After all,' she said, 'everything makes more sense in the saddle.'

I knew exactly what she meant.

'Glad you could make it, Ashleigh.' Kylie looked up briefly from her notes. She had one eye on Molly and Rebel and the other on her folder. 'Is Honey warmed up?'

I nodded. 'Yep.'

'Walk her around with the others, keep her limber.' Kylie gestured to the marshalling area, which a few months ago had been bustling with what had seemed like thousands of riders, officials and horses at the Waratah Grove Junior Cross-Country Riding Championships. It was now deserted except for the Roycrofts and their horses, all walking single file, keeping warm and ready to hit the course at a second's notice.

My heart squelched. If I'd been given a choice between being with the Roycrofts and being dental nurse to a funnel-web spider, the arachnid would have won eight legs down. But I had to think of Honey. She had to be kept moving, even if it meant negotiating icebergs more dangerous than the one that sank the *Titanic*. I slipped Honey into the line behind Lena, hoping that nobody would notice me.

'Ooh, yuck!' Brooke cried.

'What?' I twisted around.

Brooke waved her hand in front of her nose frantically. 'What's that smell? It's *disgusting!*'

'Disgusting,' said Juliette. She was holding her reins with one hand, her nose with the other.

I was confused. I couldn't smell anything. There were a lot of things at the Grove that were smelly — cows, horse poo, chickens, the Morgan boys. But apart from horse poo (which was everywhere) I couldn't figure out what was making Brooke air-vomit onto Angel's mane.

'Yuck,' she moaned between retches. 'Oh, it's just so, like, so gross. When was the last time you had a shower, Ashleigh?'

I was shocked. The only thing more shocking than Brooke turning on me like a great white at a sushi bar was that the others let her do it. Even a diver swimming in a sea full of man-eaters has a spotter, ready to fire at the first sign of bared teeth. But I was alone, no spotter and no friends.

I ignored Brooke, imagining my ears were stuffed with cotton balls and concentrated on Honey. I watched her neck bounce with every step she took.

'Adda girl,' I murmured. Her ears flicked back at the sound of my voice. I patted her firm neck and buried my fingers in her mane. 'Beautiful girl, perfect girl.'

The Roycrofts were called onto the course one by one, then sent back to cool down their horses when they'd finished their turn over the course. I was last.

'Ready?' Kylie said.

I nodded. 'You bet.'

'Go have a squiz at the first three jumps. Refresh your memory.'

I handed my reins to Kylie who stroked Honey's sweet nose then led her in wide circles. The jumps were all there, just as I remembered them. A log, a fence and a brush hut. We had taken them once before and we would take them again.

I jogged back to Kylie. She handed me my reins.

'Have they grown?'

I laughed. 'Maybe a little.'

I gathered my reins at Honey's shoulder and sprang into the saddle. I'd been looking forward to a lesson with Kylie. I had a look around. The Roycrofts were sitting on the fence, watching. Brooke and Juliette had their heads together, laughing. I was going to show them. I was going to show all of them.

'I want to see you take her over the first three

obstacles only. They're very simple. I just want to see how you handle Honey.'

'No problem,' I said, checking my girth.

Kylie frowned. 'Can you manage it?'

'Absolutely.' I gathered my reins.

Kylie raised the bell.

I prepared myself, bracing my body for what was coming. Honey's body tensed beneath me. She was waiting, too, alert and ready. My stirrups were shortened and my heels were down. My hands were low, but ready to move forward at the jump and my heart was pumping. I settled my seat and waited.

Kylie rang the bell and Honey burst into a gallop. She knew exactly what to do. We could forget about everything but the deliciousness of jumping. We churned up the long straight stretch of grass and readied ourselves for the first jump. It was there, waiting. The log. I pulled up Honey just slightly and felt her prepare to push off. I leaned forward, keeping close to the saddle and moved my hands forward as she stretched out her neck. Then we were flying! I looked down for just a second as Honey's body soared over the jump. It was all passing beneath us, the grass, the log, the shrub ... everything. This is what it was like, I thought, to ride Pegasus, the flying horse.

I felt Honey tucking up her hind legs and reaching out with her front legs. Her neck and head came up and her front feet hit the ground. I moved my shoulders and seat back a little as we landed and checked my hands, pulling Honey's head back up slightly, regaining control. Nothing else mattered! They could do anything to me, they could say anything, they could believe anything they wanted but they could never take this away from me.

We galloped on to the next jump and the next. I pulled Honey in a wide circle away from the rest of the course and cantered her back down the straight to where Kylie was waiting, her face glowing, clapping her hands just for us.

'That was brilliant, kid!' she said as we pulled up. 'I can see how you got your ticket to the Grove.'

'Really?' I asked, breathless.

Kylie patted Honey's neck and smiled up at me. 'Really. And don't you ever forget it.'

I slid to the ground and wrapped my arms around Kylie's neck. She patted my back and laughed aloud.

'What's this for?'

'Just thanks,' I whispered. 'Thanks.'

I let go of Kylie and shuffled my feet, embarrassed.

'Cool her out,' she said, adjusting her baseball cap. 'And I'll see you after Equitation.'

I led Honey to the warm-up ring and cooled her out, then put her in her stall with a haynet and a cool drink.

I wrapped my arms around her neck and held her close. I missed Shady Creek and Mum and Dad and my friends, but I had Honey and I loved her more than anyone could love a horse. What could be better than that?

EIGHT

Dressage is for Everyone

The next morning we were back in the dressage ring for our second lesson. I felt all twitchy and wriggly. My insides bubbled. The last lesson was still fresh in my mind and Brooke and Juliette seemed to be eagerly awaiting the next exciting instalment of *Ashleigh Miller's Spectacular Dressage Arena Adventures*. They actually looked hungry.

After inspection Alex approached Honey's near side. He patted her sleek neck gently and searched my face.

'Are you up for it?'

'For sure. Of course.'

Alex raised his eyebrows. 'Sounds like you're trying to convince me. Or is it you who needs persuading?'

I glanced sideways at Brooke who, in the most conspicuous example of eavesdropping I'd ever seen, was leaning so far over in the saddle I was sure she'd end up under Angel's belly.

'I'm fine,' I said loudly. 'In fact, I can't wait.'

Alex slapped Honey's neck a few times and gave me a nod. 'All righty, then.'

He perched himself on the white railing fence of the dressage ring and cleared his throat.

'I'll never figure out why so many riders find dressage intimidating, like dressage is this whole other world they'll never be a part of.'

I'd always thought that about dressage, but I was desperate to learn.

'Dressage is for everyone.'

'Except Ashleigh,' Brooke burst out. She and Juliette collapsed over their horses.

I clenched my teeth. They'd changed completely overnight. It was almost like two sweet, lovely aliens had possessed their bodies for a few days and, after realising their true natures, had run for their lives leaving nothing behind but the nasty originals. I'd woken up this morning to find my clothes chucked all over the cabin. There were no prizes for guessing who was behind it.

'Enough!' Alex barked. Brooke snapped her mouth shut. Juliette, typically, followed suit.

Honey shook her head, impatient to get moving.

'Our aim in dressage training is to have a horse and rider whose partnership is perfect and harmonious. Dressage really is simply training your horse to understand your signals.'

'What's Ashleigh's signal?' Brooke shrieked. 'Ejector seat?'

They collapsed again.

Alex reddened. 'Another remark like that and you'll be on shovel duty.'

Brooke closed her mouth and nodded, but her shoulders still shook as she tried to contain another laugh.

'Today we're going to work on our seat, to make sure we're positioning ourselves in such a way that our horses can carry our weight while responding to our most subtle aids — the signals from our hands, legs and seat. We'll also be working on some basic training exercises, brushing up for our more experienced riders and introducing the exercises to our novice riders.'

Alex beamed under his thick smear of white zinc cream. I smiled back. I was ready. He had us all dismount, stretch our legs and remount, finding our seats. Then he marched along the line of Roycrofts pushing and moulding us into the perfect dressage seat.

'You should be sitting upright in the saddle,' he said, adjusting Lena's stirrup leathers. 'I should be able to draw a line through your shoulder, hip and heel. You should have your backside in the lowest part of the saddle and your legs should be relaxed. If your muscles are tense you'll rise up.'

Alex patted Biscuit and took a few steps back. 'Now who's got a good seat happening? Ashleigh! Well done.'

I was almost weak with relief and gratitude to Holly Davis, my first riding teacher, who had been very strict about the basics. She always said I'd thank her later.

'Look at Ashleigh,' Alex said, pointing at my back. 'See the way she sits tall in the saddle. Her shoulders are relaxed, her chin is up and she's looking forward.'

'Looking forward to eating dirt!' Brooke was in hysterics now.

A shiver ran down my spine and the roots of my hair went cold.

'Shovel duty,' Alex said. 'Straight after this lesson.'

Brooke nodded. 'I'll be here.' She stared at me for a moment. There was a look in her green eyes that gave me goose bumps. 'It was worth it.'

'Everyone in the arena. We'll begin with some simple schooling. I want a half circle right then left for five minutes then serpentines for five. Get started!'

The Roycrofts filed into the arena one by one. I was so stressed by Brooke's attacks. They were getting worse. I felt wobbly, a bit like I'd swum a hundred laps of the Grove pool and followed up with fifty push-ups, but I tried to push the feeling out of my head and focus on the seat that Alex had been so wildly enthusiastic about. Brooke was taking the lead and kicked off the half circles. The other Roycrofts followed — Juliette, Lena, Tash, Molly then me.

Honey did the exercises happily, her nose to Rebel's tail, content to follow him wherever he led. I was relieved. I'd been terrified even to go near the dressage ring, much less the arena after Honey's last performance. But so far, so good. Maybe the whole thing had been a one-off.

After the serpentines, where we rode in and out, snake-like, up and down the arena, Alex had us canter in 20-metre circles (Brooke, Juliette and Lena in one; Molly, Tash and me in another), and he finished us off with an exercise called a demivolte, which was like cantering in an oval with a diagonal line slicing it down the middle.

Then it was time for our individual training. Alex set Tash, Brooke, Juliette and Lena to work on a test he had given them after the first lesson. Molly and I were sent to a quiet corner of the ring for some dressage cramming. I'd been dying to get her alone. Of all the Roycrofts, Molly had genuinely been the friendliest and the most understanding. If I could just get her to believe me, that I had nothing to do with the photo, then she could talk to Tash who'd talk to Lena and everything would be perfect. I'd still have to put up with Brooke and Juliette (who were dressed like a pair of Iced Vovos) but if I had the others on my side I could handle the gruesome twosome, no worries.

We rode together in silence. Honey was still settled, probably because Rebel refused to budge from her side.

'Look, Molly —' I began.

'I have got to talk to you,' Molly hissed, looking over her shoulder at the arena. Alex was on his way over. 'We haven't got much time.'

A jolt zapped through me. 'What?'

Molly bit her lip. 'It's Brooke. There's something you need to —'

'Girls!' Alex boomed. 'Ready to get started?'

Molly and I exchanged glances. No, we weren't. I had to know what she was about to say. I didn't think I could last through an entire lesson without knowing. Alex's timing couldn't have been worse.

'I'd like to be able to prepare the two of you for Preliminary level competition,' Alex said once we'd pulled up. 'I see your look, Ashleigh, and yes, it is possible.'

'Was it that obvious?' I said. Molly patted my hand. I beamed at her.

Alex smiled. 'Yes. Preliminary is a perfectly attainable level for you guys even though you've never done any dressage before. You'd be expected to perform a working trot, working canter, medium walk and free walk — no collected paces.'

'A working what?' Molly cried.

Alex smiled. 'Sorry, guys. A working trot is the pace between the medium and the collected trot. The horse should be balanced and have even, elastic steps. The working canter is similar. It's between the medium and collected canter and the strides are even and light.'

'And the medium walk?' I asked, all the information Alex had just delivered spinning around my head.

'It's free and energetic, but calm,' Alex said. 'And the free walk allows the horse the maximum amount of rein and a totally free head and neck.'

'Oh.' I nodded, wide-eyed.

'Easy,' Molly said.

'We'll see! You'll be working in long straight lines and large circles. No fancy stuff. But the judges will want to see free and forward movement, a good balanced seat from you and a nice obedient horse. Think you can manage that?'

'Definitely.'

'First step, lunging. Ashleigh, you're going first. Molly, take Rebel on a walk around the fence. Think about your seat and how you're holding your hands. Think about the signals you're giving Rebel with your legs. This is a free walk so his strides should be energetic but relaxed. Ready?'

'I'm onto it,' Molly said, gathering her reins. She turned to me with a huge smile, the first I'd received from a Roycroft all day. 'Good luck, Ash.'

Alex slipped a cavesson over Honey's nose and clipped a long lunge line to the centre ring on the noseband. He let out the line and fetched a whip from the fence.

'Walk her in a circle,' he said. 'Walk on!'

Honey sprang into a light free walk, her ears pricked forward. Her tail swished from side to side. We completed a few loops.

'Halt!' Alex called. Honey stopped instantly, perfectly. 'She's done this before.'

We continued with *walk on* and *halt* until Alex suggested we try a trot. Honey responded immediately to his commands.

'Relax your legs!' Alex called. 'They should be loose. Arms at right angles, hands just in front of you, about 10 centimetres. Fingers closed around the reins. We're going to try a canter now. Canter! Good!'

Lunging was a chance for me to let go. I left worrying about what Honey was doing to Alex and focussed totally on my seat, legs, back and hands. I realised that the world was a much better place when looking at it through a horse's ears.

'She's doing so well,' Alex said, once we'd halted. 'She's so responsive. I'm convinced this horse has had dressage experience. What say we let her off the lunge and into the arena?'

I was breathless from the sheer joy of the ride. Honey's hoofbeats were still pounding away inside my heart. I nodded. 'Okay.'

'I want you to walk her around the arena. I'm curious to see how she reacts now that she's settled in.'

Alex unbuckled the cavesson and patted Honey's neck, then called to Molly who trotted Rebel over to be lunged.

I rode Honey to the arena. Tash and Lena were riding side by side, Tash calling out tips and encouragement. Juliette and Brooke had abandoned the arena and were hanging over the fence talking to Rex.

We entered the arena at A. She was calm. We did a lap of the arena at a walk, then another and a third at a trot. I patted her neck, proud that she was trying so hard. Just when I thought that Honey's troubles were behind us someone rang a bell. Honey halted, stiffening so much I felt myself rise in the saddle.

'What's going on?' I cried. 'Who's doing that?'

The bell rang on and on. Honey pawed the ground, took the bit between her teeth and yanked down hard on the reins. I lost my grip and groped for them but it was too late. Honey reared, lashing out with her forelegs. I grabbed at her mane, clutching a handful as she touched down. I scrambled down from her back and snatched the dangling reins. Honey tossed her head and pulled back, reversing, dragging me along after her like a water skier. I heard a scream then Honey stopped. She'd backed straight into Lena!

'Whoa!' Alex shouted. He was in the arena in two seconds flat. 'Are you okay, Lena? What happened?'

He took hold of my reins, making soothing

noises and led Honey out of the arena and away from the dressage ring. The minute her hooves hit the cobblestones in the waiting area Honey was calm. I didn't understand it at all. How could a horse Alex believed had dressage experience behave like a lunatic every time she hit the arena? Was it me? What was I doing wrong?

My eyes stung. I knew what was coming. Hot tears spilled down my face. I brushed them away, my throat so tight and sore I knew I could barely speak.

Alex offered me Honey's reins. I took them, shaking my head.

'I have to get back in the ring,' he said. 'Cool her out and untack her.'

'I'm sorry,' I croaked. 'It won't happen again.'

Alex stroked Honey's face and sighed. 'I can't let her back in the dressage ring if she's going to rear. It's dangerous for everyone, her included. Not to mention that it's habit-forming. You don't want her rearing every time she goes near an arena.'

'Please give her another chance!' I said. 'Please, Alex.'

Alex frowned. 'I'm sorry, Ashleigh, but I can't take that kind of risk. There are five other riders in

Roycroft.' That seemed to jog his memory and he looked at his watch. 'I have to get back.'

He headed back into the dressage ring and I could hear him calling out to the Roycrofts to line up.

Frustration welled inside me. It was so unfair! Honey had been spooked by that bell; that was all. It was all right for Alex. Everyone knew he was a champion. He had nothing to prove to anyone. Honey and I did. We had to prove we could cut it at Waratah Grove. How could we face everyone back home if we messed up? I tugged at Honey's reins and walked her around the waiting area, cooling her out. She rubbed her head on my shoulders.

'Humph,' I muttered. 'Ashamed of yourself, are you? You should be!'

There were so many mysteries at the Grove. What was going on between Tash and Brooke? Why was Brooke so nasty to me all of a sudden? And what was going on with Honey? I was going to solve them all one by one, come horse or high water.

NINE

Horse Whispers

'It's true,' Molly insisted. I was grooming Honey for the tenth time that day. The stables were the only place left in the Grove where I still felt comfortable. 'I just know they set you up.'

I shrugged, running the body brush over Honey's gleaming chestnut coat. My stomach growled. I'd missed lunch but I'd opted for starving over facing the Iced Vovos. I was tired, hungry and felt like I'd just crossed the Simpson Desert barefoot.

'You know or you think?'

'I don't know for sure —'

'Aha!' I pointed my body brush at Molly.

'But the whole thing just doesn't make sense. I mean, why would you do something like that to Tash?' Molly scratched her chin. 'You don't even know her, but Brooke and Tash knew each other before they came here. I just can't get the truth from Tash. I ask her about Brooke and she seizes up like, like —'

'Like Honey in the dressage arena.'

'Exactly.' Molly realised what she'd said and blushed. 'I mean, not exactly like Honey, more like —'

I laughed. 'Don't worry about it. But I have noticed something weird going on between them.'

'And if Brooke's good enough at acting to pretend to be your friend for days, lying about the photo would be easy.'

I shivered. 'Don't rub it in.' I felt like a prize idiot. How could I have fallen for Brooke's routine? A terrible realisation dawned on me. Well, two. I'd been pretty dumb to fall for it in the first place. But even worse than that — why had she done it? She must have had a reason. What had I done wrong? I'd never met her before in my life so it couldn't have been something I'd done to her. Or could it? I ran my hand down Honey's back and over her rump.

'We have to find a way to crack them.' Molly pulled at her top lip with her fingers, thinking. 'Juliette would talk. She's a sheep. But Brooke'll be tough.'

'Forget about it, Moll,' I said. I dumped my brush into my grooming kit. 'There's nothing either of us can do. It's my word against hers.'

'How can you give up like that? I thought you were a fighter!' Molly grabbed my shoulders.

'You're not going to shake me, are you?' I asked, searching her face. 'It's just that I'm so hungry, I think I'll fall over.'

Molly grimaced. 'No, but I should. You're letting her walk all over you.'

I peered over my shoulder.

'What are you doing?' Molly folded her arms across her chest.

'Looking for footprints on my shirt.'

'Ooooh!' Molly cried, exasperated. She grabbed my hand and dragged me out of Honey's stall and to the stable door. 'Look at her!'

Brooke was sitting at the fountain laughing and talking and having a wonderful time. Three of the Morgan boys and Juliette (of course) were hanging on her every word.

'Did you rip up the photo?'

'No way.'

'Did Brooke stab you in the back?'

'You bet your saddle.'

Molly dragged me back inside. 'Listen to me! I have a plan.'

I had nothing to lose. Whatever she had in mind, I had to give it a go.

'Where are we going?' I asked. My teeth were chattering. Either I was really nervous or really cold. I was just too tired to tell.

'Shush,' Molly hissed. 'Just trust me, okay?'

I shushed. For a minute.

'But what are we doing?'

Molly pulled a face and ran her fingers along her lips, closing them zipper-style.

I held up my hands in surrender. 'Okay, I'll be quiet. I just want to know what we're doing following the gruesome twosome around in the dark.'

Molly groaned and slapped her hand over my mouth. I took the hint.

We'd watched Brooke and Juliette's every move since dinner. They'd hung around at the back of the recreation room until the movie started and then crept out when no one was looking. Now they were sneaking back towards Roycroft cabin, which was totally forbidden at night unless Kylie was there. Kylie was where I wanted to be. Curled up in a nice squishy armchair in the rec room watching *The Man from Snowy River*.

We were about five horse lengths behind Brooke and Juliette. They trotted up the cabin steps and looked around, making sure nobody was looking. Then they slipped inside.

'I knew it!' Molly said, grinning. 'They're up to something again.'

'But what are we —'

Molly's hand pressed against my mouth again. Her face was serious. 'We're going to clear your name.'

I followed Molly past the cabin and around the back. There was nothing behind the cabin but trees and shrubs and as far as I was concerned trees and shrubs equalled bugs, and lots of them.

'Have I ever mentioned that I hate spiders?' I whispered.

Molly shook her head, crouching low under a branch.

'And snakes, I hate snakes.'

Molly stopped dead and spun around.

My heart thumped. 'What? What is it? Is it a snake?'

'It's you! Be quiet! We're on a stake-out.'

I bit my bottom lip and nodded. Molly pressed on. I followed her, stepping carefully, fearfully, my hands stretching out in front of me, hoping that if I were going to walk into a spider's web it would be with my hands and not my face.

'This is it,' Molly hissed, pointing to a window. The curtains were open. Light spilled gently from the window to the ground. Someone was crouching below the window. I grabbed Molly, ready to scream for help.

Tash waved, grinning.

Molly stepped aside and Tash saw me. Her face fell.

'What's she doing here?' she demanded in a hushed voice as she came towards us.

I frowned and folded my arms. Molly had set me up. Some friend! 'I could ask the same thing,' I whispered back.

'You're the one who ripped up my photo!'

I took a step closer to her. 'You're the one who jumped to conclusions! You never gave me a chance to explain. You've never liked me from day one!'

'No friend of Brooke's is a friend of mine!'

'In case you haven't noticed, Brooke is not my friend. She never was. She was faking it.'

'I could have told you that right from the start.'

'So why didn't you? That makes you just as bad as her.'

Molly stood between us. 'This is exactly what Brooke wants. Do you guys want to find out what really happened?'

I gave a sullen nod. So did Tash.

'Good. Now the pair of you knock it off. We have a job to do.'

We crouched our way back to the window and peeked over the sill for a moment.

Brooke was talking, a mobile phone pressed to her ear.

'I thought mobiles were banned from the Grove,' I hissed.

'Brooke makes her own rules,' Tash muttered. 'Or hadn't you noticed?'

Just as I was about to bite back at her Juliette opened my bedside drawer.

'What does she think she's doing?'

'I'd say she's going through your stuff, Ash.'

Juliette held up my photo of Mum and Dad to Brooke who pointed at it and laughed. My hands curled into balls.

'That's it,' I growled. 'They're gonna cop it.'

Molly bobbed down, tugging at the back of my shirt. The three of us crouched in the shallow pool of light under the window. 'Not yet. We have to wait for them to do something bad.'

'And going through my things isn't bad?'

Molly pressed her finger to my lips. 'Not bad enough.'

'How do we even know they're gonna do something bad?' Tash slapped at her arm frantically. 'Are there any tarantulas in Australia?'

Molly rolled her eyes. 'They snuck out of the rec room, they've already broken at least a kasquillion Grove rules and —'

'Can you hear what they're saying?' Tash whispered.

I strained, but could only make out a mumble. 'Nuh. We're gonna have to listen by the window.'

'What for?' Tash grouched. 'They'll see us.'

'No they won't. The light is on and it's dark outside.'

'Very perceptive.'

I grimaced. 'They won't be able to see outside. The light will reflect off the glass. All they'll see is themselves.'

Tash pursed her lips and thought about it. 'Just be quiet! I don't want to be busted because of you.'

I gave her a salute and stood up again, taking hold of the windowsill. Tash and Molly followed suit.

'What did you say you call her?' Brooke said into the phone. 'Spiller Miller?' She laughed hysterically. 'That's a classic, Carl. Yeah, I'll pass it around. No, she sucks at dressage. You were right about everything. Her horse is a mongrel as well ... Everyone hates her. Even Tash Symon ... Oh, just a little stroke of Brooke Barnes genius ... I just ripped up this photo of her sister and made out it was Ashleigh ... Yeah, totally cool ... I promise you, Carly, as your cousin, I'll make her sorry she ever set foot in Waratah Grove.'

I was stunned, gobsmacked, mortified. I could hardly believe what I was hearing. I slid down the wall and collapsed on the ground underneath the window not caring how many bugs I landed on. Molly and Tash kept listening for a while then joined me.

'They've gone,' Molly said. 'Juliette took some sheets from your stationery set. Maybe she's going to write you a letter.'

'She can have it,' I mumbled, brushing a single tear from my face.

'Wow, Brooke's really got it in for you, hasn't she?' Tash said.

'Double wow,' Molly said. 'I've never met anyone like her.'

'I can't believe I could be so dumb,' I said. I was so mad at myself.

'What?' Molly said.

'Brooke Barnes, Carly Barnes. They're cousins!'

'Who's Carly Barnes?' Tash slapped at her arm. 'Mozzie!'

'A creep from home who's a little bit upset that I'm here and she's not. She's in my Riding Club and she totally hates me. When I won the Cross-Country Champs she couldn't handle it. So she's obviously told her cousin to make my life miserable.'

'So, Tash, do you believe her now?' Molly said. 'She didn't rip up your photo. Brooke did.'

Tash smiled sheepishly. 'Yeah, I believe you. And I'm sorry.'

'And Brooke was only pretending to be Ash's friend, to gain her trust and stop her making friends with anyone else.'

'I give up!' Tash cried, holding up her hands in surrender. 'I'm sorry! I should have given you the benefit of the doubt. I really hope we can be friends.'

'Of course we can,' I said. 'Friends.'

I held out my hand to Tash and she clasped it.

'Friends.'

Molly clapped her hands. 'That's so sweet! I knew everything would work out!'

'So, what should three stalwart friends do in a situation like this, I hear you ask.' Tash's eyes were alight.

'What?' Moll and I said together.

'Plan our revenge.' Tash cackled and rubbed her hands together. 'First, let's get out of this jungle, then . . . let's get even!'

★ ★ ★

The rec room was full of people watching the movie. The lights were off, so it was easy to slip back inside unnoticed. The three of us sat together with one eye on the screen, the other on the Iced Vovos who were back from the cabin. I wanted to burst out of my chair, grab Brooke by the shoulders and shake the curls out of her hair, but I didn't suppose that would do our revenge plan any good. So I sat there biting my tongue and punching my fist into my palm until the movie was finished and we were all sent to bed.

The Roycrofts trooped back to their cabin, Kylie promising to be along in a few minutes. Molly, Tash and I acted like nothing had changed. Tash did a great job of sending horrible looks in my direction. Molly and Lena huddled around her supportively. I curled up on my bed, biting my nails.

'We dibs first showers,' Brooke announced. 'Unless Ashleigh needs to, like, wash her hands. Got caught red-handed, eh, Miller?'

'Red-handed,' Juliette said, parrot-style.

I thought I was going to have to shove my fist into my mouth to keep quiet.

Brooke swung her towel over her shoulder and scooped up her pyjamas and toothbrush. 'Keep an eye on *her* for us, okay?' she said to the others, gesturing at me. 'I wouldn't want to come back and find anything of *mine* damaged.'

The Iced Vovos sauntered from the cabin and headed for the showers. Molly, Tash and I froze until we heard the shower door close, then we sprang into action.

'What's happening?' Lena said, baffled.

Tash knelt in front of her and looked into her eyes. 'Don't be afraid. Be a good girl and get your shower things ready. I'll be back in a minute.'

Lena was happy with that. She looked at Tash with huge, adoring eyes. 'Okay, Tasha.'

Tash opened the door. 'Let's go. We can't waste a second.'

In ten seconds we were in the shower block. In another five we each had a bundle in our arms. A few minutes later we were pushing our bundles into one of the enormous feed bins behind the stables. In another two minutes we were back in position in the cabin, our tummies aching from laughter.

'Shush!' Molly gasped. 'They'll be here before you know it.'

I wiped tears from my eyes. 'I can't wait.'

Tash's face was buried in her hands. Her shoulders were shaking. She sat up straight, cupping her ears with her hands. 'Ready?'

There was a scream. Then another and some shouting. Then some doors banged hard and bare, wet feet slapped up the cabin stairs.

The door flew open and Brooke charged inside dripping, wild-haired and wrapped in a shower curtain.

'Who stole my clothes?' she screamed. Her face was as red as sunset. Her white teeth flashed.

I curled up tighter, sure I'd give us away by laughing.

Tash peered at Brooke, looking confused. Her eyes were wide and innocent. She was brilliant. 'What happened?'

'What d'ya reckon happened? I'm standing here in a shower curtain, genius!' I thought Brooke was having a fit.

Tash shrugged. 'That's not a real bright idea, Brookey. If I were you I'd put on some clothes.'

That was the end of Molly. She collapsed in giggles.

'You, CREEP!' Brooke howled. 'I'm reporting you. I'm going to *so* get you!'

I couldn't keep my mouth shut a second longer. I got off my bed and stood in front of Brooke. 'Not if I get you first.'

Brooke's face fell slightly. She turned her green, cat-like eyes to me. They were cold and very scary.

'What is that supposed to mean?' She dropped her voice, narrowed her eyes and pulled her lips back in a malevolent sneer.

'Just suppose I accidentally let it slip that you ripped up Tash's picture and blamed it on me,' I said. 'And that you snuck in a mobile phone and that Juliette was snooping in my drawers? What do you think might happen then?'

In an instant Brooke's face changed from menacing to mindful. She thought about it for a moment, then pushed me out of the way.

'Just stay away from me,' she spat, ripping her dressing gown from her bed and grabbing Juliette's. She marched from the cabin, slamming the door behind her.

'Say hi to Carly for me!' I shrieked, thoroughly enjoying myself.

Tash, Moll and I burst out laughing. It was the sweetest of revenges.

'That should keep her out of our hair for a while,' Tash said, wiping the tears from her face. Lena bounced onto her bed and wrapped her arms around her. Moll and I dragged my bed and drawers across the room, parking them next to Tash. We were weak from giggling. It was the happiest I'd been at Waratah Grove. From that night, we were mates.

TEN

Tash to the Rescue

'Alex, that's not fair!'

Alex folded his arms and frowned up at Tash. Molly, Tash and I were mounted, warmed up and ready for dressage. 'My decision is final. Ashleigh is banned until further notice.'

'But —' I began.

'No buts, no ifs, no begging. Honey's dangerous. And until I see a complete change in her behaviour you'll have to sit out the lessons.'

Tash scowled. 'What's she supposed to do for the rest of the lesson?'

'She can start by mucking out Angel's stall,' Brooke said, arriving just in time to make a typically

Brooke remark. 'I'm gonna be too, like, busy getting ready for graduation.'

I gasped. It was like two great icy hands had taken hold of my heart and were squeezing it as hard as they could. Graduation! I'd forgotten about it. I'd been so caught up in that horrible Brooke business. But now the full weight of what could happen hit me. If I didn't go to dressage lessons I wouldn't pass my final test and if I didn't pass my final test I wouldn't graduate!

'Please, Alex, please, please, please!' I gave him my sweetest, cutest, little lost puppy dog look that always works on Dad.

Alex frowned even more and pointed at the ring gate. 'I said no begging. Cool out your horse, turn her out and watch the lesson from the stands.'

'Too bad, Miller,' Brooke said, fluttering her mascara-laden eyelashes. 'Now run along like a good girl and make sure you take plenty of notes. I'll show you how it's done.'

'Actually, Brookey's right, Ash.'

I gaped at Tash. How could she possibly be on her side after everything she'd done to us?

'She'll show you exactly how a bad rider flukes a

good score because her parents bought her a brilliant dressage horse.' Tash gave Brooke a tight smile. It was Brooke's turn to gasp.

'Are you still here, Ashleigh?' Alex called. He was sitting at the judges' table, tapping his watch.

'I'm gone!'

Tash and Molly sent me sympathetic smiles. They'd tried their hardest. There was nothing more we could do.

I cooled out and turned out Honey and sat in the stands, just like Alex said. I hated to admit it but I was glad I did. I'd never sat back and really watched a lesson — it had been pretty impossible being involved in anything other than trying to stay on Honey's back. But from the stands I saw everything in a new way. I understood more. Dressage wasn't just about riding around doing fancy steps and wearing cool clothes. It was about communicating with your horse on a level you've never communicated on before, not with anybody. I knew now about the signals, so subtle that even the sharpest eye failed to see them. I knew how responsive and athletic the horses had to be. I knew about the years of training that go into making an awesome team. As I watched Tash and Silver perform so beautifully in the arena, they appeared to be dancing. My eyes filled with tears. I wanted this so badly. I wanted Honey to trust me enough, to open her heart to me. I wanted us to be that close and look that perfect together. There had to be a way to get through to Honey. I wasn't going to give up on her. No way.

I sat between Tash and Moll at dinner that night, chewing on my thumbnail.

Tash nudged me, indicating my empty plates. We'd feasted on Mr S's home-made hamburgers with salad and chocolate pudding for dessert. I'd managed to eat faster than anyone else. That's what happens when I'm nervous. 'You still hungry?'

I shook my head. 'Freaking out.'

Molly frowned. 'What's wrong?'

I shrugged, chewing hard. I shivered although it was warm in the dining room.

'Tell us,' Tash said. 'My mum always said that a problem shared is a problem halved.'

'It's Honey. And dressage.'

Tash frowned and picked at her pudding.

'I don't need her to win anything. I've never been into dressage. Until now, that is. I just hate not knowing what's wrong with her. I hate not being allowed in the arena. And I hate looking like an idiot in front of Brooke and Alex.' I didn't tell them how I really felt about wanting to ride the way they did. I just couldn't find the words.

'She ever done anything like this before?' Tash said.

I shrugged. 'Only the plastic bag thing.' Then I told her Honey's story. About how I'd found her abandoned, sick and half-starved and how Becky and I had rescued her. About how Honey had nearly died and how I'd looked after her and finally got to keep her.

'Wow,' said Molly.

'Wow,' said Tash. 'And you won the Cross-Country Champs? That's so cool.'

'She sure did,' Molly leaned forward and picked a piece of hay out of Tash's mad hair. 'I was there, I saw it.'

'But now I'm totally stressing. There's no way I'll graduate if I can't perform a simple test.'

'No, you won't,' Tash said, scraping up her last spoonful of pudding. 'Not unless . . . I'm so brilliant!'

'Unless what?' Molly said, confused.

'Why are you so brilliant?' I added.

Tash pointed her spoon at me, her eyes sparkling with mischief. '*I'm* gonna teach you. You and Honey.'

'How? Where?'

Tash was fizzing. 'We'll hide somewhere. Anywhere. We'll sneak off and I'll teach you, then on exam day you and Honey will blitz 'em in the ring and Brookey will have the smile rubbed off her face for good. And how cool would it be for that Carly kid to hear how well you did?'

I had to smile. 'It would be *so* worth it just to see the look on her Creep face.'

'Then it's settled,' Tash said, sticking out her hand. 'Tomorrow we begin. And in three weeks you are gonna be the dressage queen of Waratah Grove.'

I bit at my bottom lip but clasped Tash's hand and shook it hard. 'You're on.'

ELEVEN

Tash's Plan

'Ready?' Tash asked.

'Sure am.' I fumbled at the buckle of my helmet, the pain of my last experience in the arena still throbbing in my butt.

'Let's make a start, then. There's nobody here now. And Alex never said you couldn't use the arena when it was empty, did he?'

'That's correct.'

Tash circled me and Honey, closely scrutinising us. She checked my feet, hands and seat, the saddle, bridle and girth straps.

'Would you like to check my teeth, as well?'

'Ha ha. I'm looking for something obvious. But I can't find anything wrong at all.' Tash shrugged and scratched her head, then checked her watch. 'You'd better get in there before they get back from the trail ride.'

Everyone was on the trail except a few Grove staff hands. We'd told Mrs S that our tummies were aching and we couldn't possibly last the whole ride. Molly had gone with Lena to minimise suspicion and keep Brooke from pecking at her like a vengeful chook.

'What do you want me to do? You're the boss.' I fidgeted with a strand of Honey's mane and sent up a frantic prayer to the horse gods. *Please, please let her be okay. Please tell her not to be afraid.*

Tash surveyed the arena. 'Just walk her in and do a lap. No point in trying anything fancy until we know she can cope on the inside.'

I shuddered. 'You make the arena sound like a prison.'

'That's how it seems to Honey.' Tash patted Honey's neck and looked up at me. 'Go.'

I squeezed Honey's middle and she walked into the arena.

'So far, so good,' Tash called.

I concentrated on Honey, ready to bail at the first sign of trouble. We passed F, then B and M. I turned Honey, using slight pressure on my left rein and shifting the weight in my seat. She obeyed. We passed C and turned towards H.

'Way to go!' Tash called.

Honey stopped suddenly and refused to go any further.

I squeezed her middle. 'Walk on, Honey, there's a girl.'

'Use your aids!' Tash cried.

'I am, I am!' I wanted to cry. I couldn't even get my horse to walk. There was no way we'd be ready in three weeks.

Tash jogged into the arena. 'Let me have a go.'

I slid to the ground and unbuckled my helmet, passing it to Tash. She put it on and mounted. I felt a twinge of jealousy. Honey was my horse. Nobody had ever ridden her but me. Not even Becky and Becky was my best friend.

Tash seemed to know what I was thinking. 'I know it's hard, Ash, watching someone else ride your horse. But it's necessary.'

'Don't be silly!' I lied. 'I'm fine. We have to do what's best for Honey.'

Tash gathered her reins. 'I'll have a go. You'd better go wait in the stands.'

I grimaced. 'Okay.'

As I turned and walked to the stands, I had no inkling anything was wrong until I heard Tash cry out. When I looked back at the arena my heart fell into my riding boots. Honey was out of control and Tash was clinging to her back. My horse spun in circles, tossing her head, then reared and jumped out of the arena. Tash pulled down hard on the reins. I trusted her. She knew what she was doing, but I was so afraid for her. And for Honey. We'd closed the ring gates so Honey had nowhere to go but she was determined. She galloped around the ring once, twice.

I ran back into the ring, holding up my hands.

'Honey, stop!' I cried. My Honey horse was wild, her eyes rolled and she reared again, only metres away from me. When she touched down I leapt forward and grabbed her reins. Tash scrambled down, shaking.

I stroked Honey's nose, trying to calm her. She was breathing hard. Her face was dirty and streaked with sweat. Tash doubled over, her hands resting on her knees.

'Tash, are you okay?'

'I'm fine,' she said, panting. 'In fact I'm now considering a career in rodeo. But Honey is not ready for the arena. We need to find somewhere else to train her.'

I was shocked. 'You still want to help me?'

Tash smiled. 'Of course. Why wouldn't I?'

'But Honey was so ... so ...' I swallowed hard. 'So naughty!'

'You think I'd let that stop me? My mum always said that a friend in need is a friend indeed.' Tash unbuckled my helmet and fluffed out her hair. It stuck straight up, out and everywhere else. She patted Honey's neck. 'What a gorgeous girl.'

I was amazed. Anyone else would have run for the nearest rocking horse. Except maybe Becky.

'Don't worry,' Tash said. 'We'll think of something.' She looked at her watch again. 'Let's get out of here before we get busted.'

'Sounds good to me.'

We cooled out, untacked and rubbed Honey down, removing all traces of the saddle.

'She'll have a roll, I bet. No one will ever know we were in the ring.' Tash patted Honey's rump as we turned her out. Tash was right. The first thing Honey did was find the dustiest, driest patch of paddock she could and rolled. So much for grooming!

There was a burst of sudden activity from the stables. Tash and I jogged over to investigate.

Mrs S bore down on us leading her stunning grey, pink-nosed Arab mare, Aliyah.

'I hope you two ladies have made a full recovery.'

Tash clutched her stomach. 'It was touch and go for a while there, Mrs Strickland.'

A faint smiled tugged at Mrs S's lips. She liked Tash, I could tell. Whether or not she liked me or not was still hard to say.

'Very well. Now get away with you, unless you're in the mood for some dishwashing.'

We scampered off in search of Molly.

At dinner, Molly, Tash and I stuck our heads together. Molly had good news.

'It's like a clearing, just off the trail we took today.'

'Won't we get caught?' I peered across the table at Brooke and Juliette. Thankfully they were ignoring us.

'There won't be anyone on the trails during the week,' Tash hissed. 'You'll get a few on the weekends but that still gives us almost three weeks' training.'

'But how are we gonna get away?'

Tash waved her hand at me as though getting away from the Grove with Honey completely unnoticed was going to be the easiest thing in the world. 'Leave it to me.'

TWELVE

Honey's Secret

'This is perfect.' Tash surveyed the clearing. It seemed to have been custom made by nature for dressage training. The whole area was flat and rectangular and almost completely surrounded by trees and shrubs. Nobody would find us unless they knew exactly where to look.

'Is Molly covering for us?'

'I told her to say we'd gone on a hike around the farm if anyone asks. Who'd wanna traipse around in all that cow poo looking for us?' Tash looked at her watch.

'You'd better climb aboard. You know we don't get much leisure time.'

I'd doubled Tash to the clearing on Honey. Silver needed rest after the morning's workout. Honey, on the other hand, needed schooling.

I sprang into the saddle while Tash jogged around the clearing placing white upturned plastic cups where the markers should be.

'Brilliant idea!' I was impressed.

Tash fluttered her eyelashes. 'Why, thank you, ma'am.'

I leaned forward and whispered to Honey, words only she could hear. I asked her to be brave and strong and to believe in me. I would never hurt her, ever. I loved her and together, we could do anything.

'Free walk into the arena A to C, chuck a left and walk back H to K.' Tash settled onto a fallen log.

'*Chuck a left*? Is that correct dressage terminology?' I giggled.

Tash rolled her eyes. 'Just do it. And remember that the key to it all is free and forward movement!'

I took a moment to find the perfect dressage seat and squeezed Honey's middle. She walked perfectly. I hoped she was free and forward. At least she wasn't rearing, bolting or reversing.

'She looks great, you know. Why don't you try her at a collected walk instead?'

'Alex said I don't need to —'

'But Alex isn't here, is he? Try her. Best to start collecting her at the corner. She already has to bring her inside hind leg further underneath her there.'

I gritted my teeth, but obeyed. I used half-halts, reining Honey in with my hands while keeping pressure on her sides with my legs. As we turned on to the straight I applied more pressure to Honey's sides until I felt the shorter, higher steps of collection, then I released the pressure on her mouth.

'Good one, Ash!' Tash clapped from her log. 'I didn't know you had it in you!'

I smiled. 'You have so much to learn, Natasha.'

Tash scowled. 'Move to the trot, same direction. Then I want a canter.'

'As you command!'

Honey moved easily into a collected trot and after two laps, a collected canter. On our second circuit I lost control of my seat for a moment and shifted. I felt what seemed like Honey stumbling and pulled her up.

I looked at Tash. 'What happened?'

Tash was staring at us, her mouth open in a large O. 'What happened? What happened? Are you serious?'

I shrugged, mystified. 'Yeah, what happened?'

Tash stood up on her log and raised her hands in praise to the horse gods. 'That was a flying change! Honey just did a flying change!'

'A what?'

Tash was effervescent. 'I know a flying change when I see one and Honey just did one!'

She dashed over and grabbed Honey's bridle, searching her face. 'What was her name, before you got her?'

I grimaced. 'Argonaut.'

Tash ran her hands down each of Honey's legs and took a few paces back, taking her in. 'Argonaut, Argonaut. Hmm. It's ringing bells.'

'What is the matter with you, Tash?' I slid to the ground and grabbed her hand.

'Don't you see? This isn't any ordinary horse. This is a dressage horse! No horse would do a flying change just for the heck of it. They need years of training. And hers was perfect. Like you'd see in any top-level competition.'

I was confused. 'So why is she freaking out in the arena? Why isn't she doing flying changes in front of Alex?'

'I don't know. But I can tell you this. First, we'd better get back to the Grove. Secondly, we have homework to do.'

I scrambled onto Honey's back and pulled Tash up behind me.

'I told you!' Tash poked at the computer screen. We were online, digging for clues.

'I can't believe it. The answer has been here, all the time.' I slumped in my chair, stunned.

It was there in black and white — an article on the screen describing the lifetime ban of a rider for whipping her horse repeatedly across the head after a poorly performed dressage test. The horse, a chestnut mare, had sustained serious injuries. Her name was Argonaut.

'No wonder,' Tash said, shaking her head in disbelief. 'It's got nothing to do with you at all, Ash. Honey is so traumatised she doesn't like being in the dressage arena.'

'It's disgusting.' I was in shock. 'First they beat her

up then they starve her. Some people just don't deserve horses.'

'I knew it. The second you told me what Honey was called by *those* people.' Tash said 'those' like it was a dirty word. 'I heard about it at a show two years ago. Everyone was upset.'

I buried my face in my hands feeling hot tears prick at my eyes. How could she have done it? To my Honey? Honey was so sweet. How could anyone do a thing like that to a horse? It didn't make any sense. I felt Tash's hand on my back, patting me gently. She understood. If it had happened to Silver she would have been as heartbroken as I was. All I wanted to do was go to Honey and hug her, tell her how much I loved her and promise her that nothing or nobody would ever hurt her again.

'You okay?' Tash asked, logging off.

I nodded. I couldn't speak.

'Let's go and see how your girl is doing. You look like you could use a horsy hug.'

Tash stood up, rolled her chair away with a kick of her foot and held out her hand. I clasped it and she hauled me to my feet, slipping her arm around my shoulders.

'Don't worry,' she said as we made our way to the stables. 'We'll get you and Honey ready for graduation.'

'I don't care about graduation. It doesn't matter any more.' I brushed away the tears that rolled down my face.

'What do you mean, it doesn't matter?' Tash stopped in her tracks and regarded me. 'Of course it matters. How can it not matter?'

'Think about it, Tash. Honey was abused. She can't go into the arena and I'm not going to force her. I'd rather pack up and leave today than put her through that.'

Tash shrugged. 'I suppose you're right.'

We continued towards the stables in silence. I sped up, anxious to see Honey. She was in her stall, munching contentedly on a haynet. I slipped into her stall and bolted the door behind me. Honey turned and nickered softly. She stretched out her nose to me, nuzzling my hands and took a step toward me. I wrapped my arms around her neck and stroked her sleek coat again and again. She rubbed her head against my shoulder.

I broke away from her and held her face, running

my hands over her cheeks, forehead and nose, searching. It didn't take long to find what I was looking for. I couldn't believe I'd never noticed it before. A scar, as long as my finger, was right there behind her ear.

'Look at this,' I muttered. Tash entered the stall and squinted at the scar. 'It's been there all this time. I should have noticed. I should have known.'

'How could you know? Who would even think that their horse had been beaten like this?'

Everything started to swirl in my head. Honey, the scar, her terror in the ring, my fears about graduating, Brooke and Juliette ... it all turned and tumbled around and around until I felt sick.

I shook my head. 'I have to get out of here.'

Tash stepped out of my way. 'Where? Where are you going?'

I tugged at the bolt and pushed open the stall door. Then I ran. I ran and ran as fast as I could and didn't stop until I found myself at Mrs S's office. I pounded on her door again and again until at last, with a very sour look on her face, she opened it. I stood there, breathing hard, my face stained with tears.

Mrs S's face softened.

'I suppose you'd better come in, Miss Miller,' she said, standing aside.

I took a step inside and she closed the door behind me.

'Sit,' she said, indicating a chair.

I did as I was told and felt instantly calmer. It could have been the soft music drifting from the old radio on the filing cabinet or the dozens of photos of children, former Grovers, and her own children and grandchildren (I recognised a toothless Rex) that lined the walls of the room. Or it could have just been being with Mrs S. I realised then that she was a very calm person. I liked being around her.

Mrs S disappeared behind me. I looked around the room, fascinated. There was a framed photo on her desk — an old photo of a young woman with a stunning black horse. Ribbons lined the walls, medals were hung over everything, trophies bulged from the trophy cabinet. Books stood in long straight rows. There was a model horse collection on the very top of the bookshelf and next to Mrs S's desk there was a gorgeous painting of a black horse. Mrs S placed a glass of water in front of me. I sipped at it.

'Thank you.'

Mrs S settled into her chair. 'What can I do for you?'

I spilled the whole story, bursting into tears again and begged to be allowed to quit. I didn't care about graduating any more.

Mrs S sat back in her chair. She looked like someone who understood.

'I was hoping you'd learn of Honey's past,' she said at last. 'It was important for you to know. All horse owners need to know so that they can understand their horses, help them.'

My mouth dropped open and I stared, flabbergasted, at Mrs S. 'You *knew*?'

'Yes. I knew. I was there that day. I issued the lifetime ban.' Mrs S put her fingertips to her lips for a moment. 'The only time I've ever had to use that particular penalty.'

'Why didn't you tell me?' It was hard to say what was more shocking — learning about what had happened to Honey or learning that Mrs S had known all along.

'I took measures to protect Honey. I disallowed her from continuing in the dressage programme.'

'But you should have told me!' I flushed, embarrassed by my tone. 'Mrs Strickland.'

'You needed to learn this for yourself, Ashleigh. You needed to learn how to read your horse. And you did. And you became a better rider and a better horsewoman for it.'

'Some horsewoman. I pushed her. I hadn't even noticed her scar. I hadn't even tried to find out about her life before I found her. About what happened to her.' I stared at my hands, wringing them.

'From what I've heard, you were too busy saving her life.'

I looked up quickly. Mrs S smiled.

'Amanda Filano, your vet, is a very good friend of mine. And a very big fan of yours, Miss Miller.'

I chewed on my bottom lip and met Mrs S's eyes. 'I still think I should leave. Honey needs care. She needs help.'

'I think we can arrange a little help for your Honey,' Mrs S said. 'Besides, you've already begun some work with Miss Symon. I see no reason why that should stop.'

'You know about that too?'

'There's not a lot that happens around here that I don't know about, Miss Miller.'

I laughed, despite myself.

'Now go on with you. I believe you're running late for dinner.'

I glanced at the clock on the wall — six fifteen. Boy, was I late. I shot to my feet and made a dash for the door.

'Mrs Strickland?'

'Hmm?'

'That woman in the photo, with the black horse —'

'Yes, it's me.'

'And the horse, in the painting?'

'It's him.' She touched the portrait tenderly.

'What was your horse's name?'

'Ebony.'

'Mrs Strickland?'

'Yes?'

'Thank you.'

'You're welcome, Miss Miller.'

I closed the office door behind me and bolted to the dining hall where my friends were waiting for me.

THIRTEEN
Poles Apart

Tash and I went to the clearing the next day and the next. At every training session Honey improved. And every day she surprised me.

'I had no idea I'd been riding a champion dressage horse the whole time.' I swished at a fly that was determined to set up camp on my nose. 'I can't wait to try her in a real competition. I can't wait for the Creepketeers to see her in action.'

'I'd love to have another go,' Tash said. 'To see what she can really do.'

I unbuckled my helmet and passed it to Tash who wasted no time in springing into the saddle. I was nervous. The last time she'd ridden Honey had been a disaster, but at least there'd been a fence and a gate. There was nothing out here to stop Honey from bolting back home to Shady Creek.

'I'm gonna try a shoulder-in. It's something any dressage horse worth her chaff should be able to do.'

I was baffled. It was like Tash was speaking another language. I made a mental note to prep her on my horse riding career so far.

'Her inside foreleg should pass and cross in front of her outside leg. Her hindquarters should be straight while her forehand is flexed.'

I stared at her, open-mouthed. Tash sighed.

'Okay, okay. She should look like she's about to turn in a circle, but be going in a straight line.'

I smiled. 'Thank you, Dressage Master.'

Tash gathered her reins. 'Let's go, Honey, my girl!'

I settled onto Tash's log. Honey looked at me as if to say, *What are you doing over there? If you're there, who's on me?*

'It's okay, Honey. Just listen to Tash.'

Tash urged Honey into a walk. Honey obeyed. Now that she was away from the arena, she had no problem doing what was asked of her.

'A shoulder-in takes a while to learn, but you should be able to give it a go. I'll begin to ask her to do it as we come out of the corner. That way she's already started to bend.' Tash looked straight ahead, concentrating hard. 'I start her in a circle then use my outside hand to stop her going on with the circle while my inside leg keeps her moving forwards in a straight line and my hips stay parallel with her shoulders. See!'

I was amazed. Honey was doing a shoulder-in.

'I'm gonna try a half-pass, now. If she can do that I'll eat my helmet.'

'As long as you don't eat mine,' I said. 'I only just got that a few months ago from Santa.'

'The half-pass is a logical progression from the shoulder-in.' Tash caught my eyes and laughed. 'I mean, it starts in the same way so it's better to try it now rather than try a move that's totally different.'

'Much better,' I said, shifting on my log. It was a lot less comfortable than the saddle and my backside was beginning to throb.

'If she's the dressage queen I think she is she should move diagonally across the arena. Okay, I start her with another shoulder-in then bring my outside leg behind the girth and release my inside leg. Here she goes!'

I jumped up from my log, clapping. I wished Becky were here to see this. I'd always watched her from the sidelines when it came to dressage. I couldn't wait for her to see Honey in action.

'What else are you going to do?' I said, bubbling.

Tash pulled Honey up and patted her neck. 'Nothing. She's been out of training for a long time. I don't want to push her; she'll be sore and stiff. She needs to be eased back into it. A horse needs to be very supple to do these exercises — it's like horse gymnastics.'

I was disappointed. 'But everyone else's horse is doing it.'

Tash slid to the ground. 'Silver's up to it. I train four times a week. Molly's only just starting and even Brooke's not stupid enough to push Angel. Just trust me, okay?'

I nodded, taking Honey's reins. 'Okay.'

'Anyway, it's nearly lunchtime and I'm starved.'

I mounted and reached down to help Tash scramble up behind the saddle. 'You shouldn't be for long.'

'Why's that?'

'You're eating your helmet, remember?'

Over the next week things didn't change much. Tash kept training me and Honey in our secret clearing and the Iced Vovos spent their free time trying to make my stay at the Grove as memorable as possible. They wrote a love letter to a boy called Nathan in Morgan and signed it from me. They hung all my underpants across the tennis court net with pegs and rubbed Vaseline on my reins. Of course I didn't see them doing any of these things, but it didn't take a genius to work out who it was. They usually gave themselves away by making sure they saw my reaction first-hand and collapsing in hysterics.

Luckily for me I had much bigger things to worry about than the Iced Vovos. Graduation. It was a week away and I still hadn't made it back into the dressage ring. I was doing well enough to pass show-jumping at my level and I was blitzing cross-country. But none of that mattered. With a big fat ugly zero points for dressage I could kiss my certificate of graduation and all the prestige that went along with it goodbye. I couldn't face anyone in Shady Creek without it. It was official. Honey and I would have to move in with Jenna. I couldn't see a problem really. Other than that Jenna lives in the city in a three-bedroom apartment on the fourth floor.

After warming up, the Roycrofts gathered in the showjumping ring for our lesson with Joanne.

'Does anyone have any questions about the trial?' Joanne said after inspection. We were mounted on our horses and ready for anything.

I raised my hand. 'Are we all doing the same course?'

'Sort of. You'll all take on a course of up to nine jumps and eleven efforts.'

I waved my hand in the air. 'What's an effort?'

'Whenever your house leaves the ground,' Joanne said. 'There are six Roycrofts jumping at three different levels. We have one A-grad jumper, Tash, and she'll jump at heights of up to a metre. Molly, Lena and Juliette who are B-grade will jump up to 80 centimetres. And you and Brooke will be jumping at C-grade so you'll be jumping up to 60 centimetres.

Brooke gasped. 'I'm not a C-grade jumper. No way! And even if I was I would, like, rather fail than compete against *her*!' Brooke pointed her crop at me. She was shaking.

Joanne was unimpressed. 'So don't ride. We can't change the system that has always worked perfectly well at the Grove for just one rider.'

Brooke seethed but shut her mouth. She didn't like Joanne but knew better than to say what was on her mind, so she turned her green cat eyes on me. I could have sworn lasers were shooting from them.

'What marks will we get?' Lena asked. Biscuit gave an almighty shake and Lena clung to her saddle giggling.

'You'll be marked according to how well you jump — that is — the number of jumps you clear without knocking rails down and your time. You also need to remember to salute the judge and jump the course in the right order.'

'How do we know the right order?' I asked. I was confused. I'd learnt so much at Waratah Grove I was sure my brain had reached its peak. It was a good thing Honey was paying attention. Her ears were forward and alert. She was watching Joanne intently. If she'd had thumbs and a pen I'm sure she'd have been making notes.

Joanne smiled. 'All the jumps will be numbered on the right-hand side. There'll also be flags, red on the right, white on the left — they'll help you keep going in the right direction. And don't forget you'll walk the course first. Your horse isn't allowed to see it, though!'

Joanne looked at her watch. 'Practice jump, everyone. Quick sticks!'

I patted Honey's neck and gathered my reins, relieved to be in the saddle. It wasn't long before I was lost in Honey, in her stride and her sweetness. When we were finished I joined the Roycrofts again, Molly on one side, Tash on the other. Lena stuck close to Tash's other side.

Joanne was talking about the fences. I tried to concentrate. It was hard with all my worries about graduation.

'On the approach your body should be in the normal position, but at the take-off you should lean forward taking the weight off your seat bone and into your thighs, knees and heels. Just the same as when you jumped the cavaletti.'

'Okay, okay. When can we jump?' Brooke fidgeted in the saddle.

'When I think you're ready. And after what I saw in the last lesson, that won't be for a while yet.'

Brooke looked like she'd swallowed a fly.

'Your hands should be light on the horse's mouth. If you feel nervous, you're best to get a neck strap on now, like Lena, rather than jab your horse in the mouth later on.'

'Neck straps are for babies,' Brooke announced.

'Babies,' Juliette said.

Lena sat up tall in the saddle. 'And people who jab their horses in the mouth. Like you did last time, Brooke. Remember?'

Tash cheered. 'Let's go, Lena! Let's go!'

'Enough!' Joanne said. She indicated a single triple bar straight fence — a fence made of three poles placed on top of each other — set up beside the cavaletti. 'Nobody sets hoof on the course until the end of the week. Today we jump that over and over again and next lesson we try a spread fence over and over again. When I'm satisfied you can have a go at the course.'

I couldn't wait!

'Lena, you first.' Joanne shooed everyone back. Lena swelled with pride.

She checked her stirrups and patted Biscuit's neck then moved her into position. The jump looked enormous from where I was sitting but Lena wasn't fazed at all. She was one of the best riders I'd seen anywhere and could have beaten almost anyone from Shady Creek Riding Club with her eyes closed, one hand tied behind her back and balancing a bowl of fruit on her head. Slight exaggeration. But she was a great jumper and nobody could argue with that.

Lena cantered Biscuit in a wide circle, then pulled her towards the jump, reining her in slightly on the approach. She sat perfectly in the jumping position as Biscuit took off and soared over the fence, landing light and neat on the other side. Joanne, Tash, Molly and I cheered. Brooke just looked sour and Juliette, not surprisingly, did likewise.

Tash had a turn, then Molly and Juliette. For a shadow who never did anything unless Brooke told her to, Juliette wasn't a bad jumper. I didn't like her, but I had to give her that.

'Ashleigh, you're up.'

'Go, Ashleigh, go, Ashleigh!' Tash chanted.

'Let's hear it for our one-woman cheer squad!' Joanne said, smiling.

I urged Honey into the starting position and checked my seat, making sure that I was perfectly balanced and sitting up straight with that imaginary line that all instructors love going from my shoulder to my hip and then to my heels.

'Great seat, Ash,' Joanne said, nodding and smiling.

'Pass it on to Alex for me?' I was desperate to get back into the dressage class.

'When you're ready.'

'Yawn, yawn,' Brooke sang. 'I still have to have a turn, Miller.'

I let her words tumble over me, but not affect me, then readied myself for the jump.

Honey moved into a trot, then a light canter. I turned her wide, in the same circle Lena had carved out in the surface of the ring then pulled her towards the fence. She cantered on, her head held high, her ears forward and alert. The jump was 20 metres away, then 15. I deepened my seat, moved my shoulders forward and closed my legs against Honey's sides. Five metres to go. Honey took a few more strides and I closed my knees in tight, and just as I raised my hands Honey pushed off with her hind legs, tucking her forelegs into her chest. We floated for a second, light and balanced and all too quickly she stretched out her forelegs and touched down. We cantered away from the jump and pulled up in front of the Roycrofts. I didn't care what Brooke said. I didn't care about anything but Honey and that feeling — that feeling of flying on horseback, being one with my horse as she cut through the air with her body.

Joanne approached us, smiling. 'Good job.'

I walked Honey in circles, cooling her out. The lesson had been fun and we'd jumped well. Joanne had been happy and assured me that if we jumped the same way on trial day we'd have no problems passing. That made me feel a bit better, but I was still panicking about dressage. How was I going to pass if Alex wouldn't let me in the ring?

FOURTEEN

Truth Hurts

It was free time and while Molly brushed the knots out of Lena's long brown hair, Tash and I headed straight to the library. I'd been pretty slack in the family communication department, I know, but I'd never been so busy. Mum had sent me an email just a few days earlier thanking me for all the lovely long letters and commenting on how wonderful it was to see that I was getting good use out of Gran's stationery set. I took the hint. It was time for an emailing session of never-before-seen proportions.

There were four computers hooked up to the Net and we grabbed two of them, checking and reading our emails and sending as many as we could.

'Who are you writing to, Tash?' I asked after a while as I typed in Jenna's address.

'Em.'

'She your only sister?'

Tash grunted. 'Nuh.'

'She's pretty special to you then, eh, Tash?'

'Hmm. Yeah, you could say that, yeah.' Tash peered over her computer at me and raised one dark eyebrow. 'What's this all about? Thinking of a career in private investigation?'

'Course not!' I laughed. 'Just curious.'

I was. Terribly curious. So curious it was making me itch. There was so little I knew about Tash and so much I wanted to know. Whenever we were together we talked about Honey and dressage and riding and not a lot else. I had to find out more about her. Molly was no real help. She'd only met Tash on our first day at the Grove, the same day as me.

Why was Tash's sister Emma so special? Why did she put her photo up on the wall and talk to it, and why was she so upset when it was ripped up? I mean, it was just a photo after all, and something that could be replaced. And why did she hate Brooke so much? I still hadn't found out and we'd been hanging out together now for nearly two weeks.

'Tell me about your family,' I said, trying to sound casual. It wasn't easy.

'Not a lot to tell. There are the boys, Jesse and Shane. They're the oldest and, man, their heads are huge. Jesse just got his licence so he reckons he's Mark Skaife. Then there's me. Then Cassie, then Em.'

'Five of you?' I was shocked. I'd never met anyone from a family of five kids before. 'Must be fun, all those kids.'

'It's never boring.'

'My mum's pregnant,' I said in a half whisper.

Tash laughed. 'You're telling me!'

'I've always wanted a sister. My whole life.' I sighed, resting my chin in my hands. 'It was always so quiet at home, especially in the city. Mum and Dad were always at work and most of the time it was just me. A sister would have been unreal.'

'You don't sound very enthusiastic now.' Tash studied my face.

I've never been very good at hiding my feelings.

'It's just that ... it's just, Mum and me and ... the new baby.'

Tash smiled. 'Three's a crowd, eh?'

I couldn't have put it better. All my life it has been me and Mum and Dad, and I'm used to it. But in a few months they'll be holding the new baby, and I'll be watching from the sidelines.

'Yeah,' I said. 'Something like that. Sounds like you've got new baby experience.'

'Em's the newest. She's three now.'

'Can she read?'

'No,' Tash said, smiling.

'So why are you writing to her then?'

'Cass will read it to her. Usually I send her drawings.'

I knew a bit more, but not as much as I wanted, needed, to know. Tash was like an uncharted sea, full of mystery.

'What're your mum and dad like?'

Tash smiled gently. 'Dad's great.'

'And your mum?' I clicked on send and my email vanished into cyberspace.

Tash said nothing. I looked up at her. There was a strange look on her face; it had darkened, like a storm cloud darkens a bright sky by parking in front of the sun. Suddenly I wished I'd never asked.

'Tash?' I said. 'Are you okay?'

Tash nodded. 'Yeah. It's just that sometimes, just when I feel I'm forgetting, someone says something or I see something or I hear something and it reminds me and I feel like I haven't gotten anywhere.'

I was lost. 'Tash, what do you mean?'

Tash looked into my eyes. Hers filled with tears. 'Mum died, Ash. Two years ago. I don't tell many people. I don't like talking about it.'

I felt so ashamed. Here I was feeling miserable about having a new baby and . . . I couldn't bear to think about it. My face burned and I started to sweat. I should never have pushed her to talk. I looked at Tash, whose face was wet with tears because of me. I should have tried to comfort her, but I didn't know what to say.

'Don't worry, Ash. You didn't know.' Tash wiped her face with her sleeve.

'I should have,' I said softly. 'Molly should have told me.'

'She doesn't know either. Nobody here does, except Mrs S and you.' Tash's eyes narrowed and she coughed. 'And *Brooke*.' She said Brooke's name like it was a dirty word.

'Brooke? But how?'

'I don't wanna go there, Ashleigh.'

'Tash, I'm sorry, I —'

'If it isn't Ash and Trash.'

I spun my chair around and groaned. The Vovos stood behind us. Brooke had her hands on her hips. Juliette did likewise.

'So,' Brooke sneered. 'The two best friends. Don't they, like, look so cute together?'

Juliette whooped. 'So cute.'

'Not now, Brooke,' I said through clenched teeth. The kid couldn't have picked worse timing.

'Have you ever seen Tash's baby sister, Juliette? I mean, the real thing, not the photo.' Brooke leaned over and spoke softly in Tash's ear. 'You know, the photo we, like, cut up into a thousand tiny —'

Tash pushed back her chair and lunged at Brooke. At first I did nothing, shock seeping through my body. Then, as these things do, the next week, our last week, flashed in front of my eyes and I saw Tash being expelled from the Grove all because of the Vovos. It wasn't worth it. She had had worked so hard. Out of all of us Tash was the one who deserved to graduate the most. She had what it took to be a star and she could lose it all because of Brooke.

I grabbed a handful of her joddies and hauled her back. She thrashed, shouting lots of words at Brooke that I was never allowed to say.

Brooke blew us a kiss and skipped out of the library. It was like a slap in the face. I'd never met anyone like her. She left her Creep cousin for dead.

Tash shook me off. She was shaking with rage. She paced up and down again and again, muttering and kicking the back of the chair.

I took her by the shoulders, forcing her to look at me. 'What is going on?' I had to know. They had a history and Tash couldn't keep it from me any longer. 'You have to tell me the truth.'

Tash sank into her chair and toyed with the mouse.

'Well?' I said. I wasn't going to let up. She had to spill the beans.

'You know my sister, Emma,' Tash said slowly.

I nodded.

Tash's eyes moistened. She blinked and rubbed at them with the backs of her hands.

'Tash, please!' I was desperate.

'Since Mum died, I've looked after her. Jesse and Shane aren't interested and Cass is too young and Dad has to work. So she stays with Nanna during the day and after school she comes home with me.'

'Tash, I don't get it. What has this got to do with the photo?'

Tash shook her head. 'I miss her, that's all. I'm the one who makes her breakfast. I'm the one who bathes her and puts her to bed. I nearly didn't come here because of Em, but she gave me the photo and told me to kiss it goodnight. She has one of me next to her bed so I can get my goodnight kiss.'

'What about Brooke?' I wanted to shake it out of her.

Tash smiled weakly. A tear ran down her face. 'Brooke ...' She rubbed her eyes again then cleared her throat. I could tell she was trying really hard to stay in control. My heart was in my mouth.

'Brooke and I were in riding club together. She acted like my friend at first. Just like she did with you. We were competing in local comps. When she was winning it was okay. But once I started winning she turned nasty.'

Tash pulled out her ponytail and her hair frizzed up instantly into a huge disco ball. 'When Mum died I dropped out of comps for a long time. I just didn't care any more. And Em was just a baby. I had to look after her. When I went back to competing Brooke was furious. She said Mum dying was the best thing that ever happened to her. I made it to the Grove because I swore I would never let her win another competition.'

I'd had enough. I was sick of Brooke. I was sick of Juliette. We only had just over a week to go until graduation and I was sure of one thing. The Iced Vovos were going to get a big, nasty helping of everything they'd been serving up. And I was going to be the one to make sure they took the full dose.

FIFTEEN

Wipeout!

'She's doing so well. I can't believe the change in her.' It was Thursday, dressage lesson day, and I was desperate to get back in the arena.

To think that in the beginning I could barely get her to walk without her rearing! I ran my hand down her firm amber neck again and again. We'd done all of Tash's exercises on our own with no refusals and no fear. 'I'm so proud of her. She's really trying hard.'

'Okay,' Tash said. She pushed herself off her log and dusted down her joddies. 'We're going to try something new.'

I was ready. 'Anything!'

Tash grinned. I could tell she had something challenging in mind. 'I know she can already do this. The problem is she was doing it when you didn't want her to. I want to teach you the rein back.'

I shuddered. Honey knew how to do it, all right. That's why we were training secretly in a clearing instead of in the dressage ring with everyone else.

Tash thought for a moment. 'The rein back is asking a horse to walk backwards. It's only ever done at a walk although we both know Honey can do it at a full run.'

'Don't remind me,' I said sourly.

'Honey should be calm and relaxed.'

I leaned forward and examined Honey's face. She looked pretty calm. 'So far so good.'

'Okay, now squeeze both legs against her sides but keep pressure on her mouth.'

Honey raised her head but did nothing.

'Lift your seat bones off the saddle!'

I obeyed and Honey took a step backwards.

'That's it! You've got it. Keep up the pressure.' Tash looked ready to do a cartwheel. Her hair was practically standing on end.

Honey walked back calmly. It was wonderful. I

knew then that she truly trusted me. I knew then that she was ready.

'Okay, give with the reins and keep the pressure on her sides. She should walk forward. You did it!'

I felt like we'd won a gold medal but I couldn't help wishing there'd been someone here to see it. Someone like Alex.

Tash approached us, a wide smile lighting her face. 'She's ready for the ring.'

'Yes!'

We high-fived. Tash pulled her helmet down over her head and sprang onto Honey's back, settling in behind the saddle. She wrapped her arms around my waist and I gathered my reins, tapping my heels against Honey's sides. As we left the clearing I turned, taking one last look. The worst was behind us. The only way to go now was forward — into the dressage ring, into the arena and onto the Waratah Grove Honour Board. We were going to graduate.

After lunch I turned up to the lesson with the Roycrofts. Alex gave me a broad smile.

'Here to watch?' He wrinkled his zinc-covered nose.

I shook my head. 'Here to train. Honey is warmed up and I'm ready.'

Alex frowned. 'I haven't been notified. As far as I'm concerned you're still ringside.'

Brooke was glowing. She was so happy her skin was shining. I'd never seen anyone take so much pleasure in another person's pain.

'Please, Alex.' I lowered my voice so that Brooke couldn't hear me beg. I could feel a sticky lump rising in my throat and hot itchy tears stinging my eyes. 'I have to do this. I've been working so hard.'

Tash edged closer. 'It's okay, Alex. She can do it.'

He looked from one of us to the other and raised his hands in surrender. 'You win. But Honey's out at the first sign of trouble. Fair enough?'

I nodded, desperate to seal the deal before he changed his mind.

Alex started the lesson. The Roycrofts had been working on a test in my absence. For the final tests they'd been graded from A-level to C-level, just like in jumping. Tash and Brooke were going head to head at A. Lena and Juliette were B-grade and Molly was a C. I would have been happy to be Z-grade just as long as I could have a crack at the final test.

No test, no graduate, no Honour Board, no go home. It was too scary even to think about.

'This is the last time you'll be able to practise the test. We don't want the horses memorising the sequence. When that happens they anticipate the next movement and forget about following your instructions. Not to mention they make it a lot easier for lazy riders.'

I snuck a sideways peek at the Iced Vovos.

'It's up to all of you to memorise your test and be prepared. The dressage finals are a week away and I want each of you to do me proud!'

A week until the final tests! Then I'd be home in Shady Creek. I'd be back at school. I'd be sleeping in my own bed. I'd be hanging out with Becky and calling Jenna and everything would be the same as ever. Or would it? There was the small issue of the new baby. There wasn't long to go now until my whole life changed forever and there was nothing I could do about it.

Alex inspected us, giving Honey an extra pat, and sent Tash into the arena to practise her test. Brooke had the job of watching for mistakes. She was delighted to report that Silverado had not maintained the correct bend in the half-pass and that he had worked on four tracks instead of three in the shoulder-in. Tash returned the favour by drawing Alex's attention to Brooke's sloppy hands, her failure to smile and the fact that she had been riding Angel at a medium trot instead of a collected one. They glared at each other as they passed. Alex was oblivious.

'Next up, B-grade!' he said. Lena and Juliette readied themselves.

Once they were finished it was Molly's turn. Her test was simple — entering the arena and saluting the judge, walking, riding at a working trot and halting. Her performance was perfect and I was happy for her. Rebel was going to make an amazing dressage horse.

Alex looked to me. 'You ready to give it a bash?'

'I'll give it a go as long as we can leave the bash out of it.'

Alex laughed. 'Very funny. Do you think you can do what Molly did?'

'You bet!'

Honey and I had been riding in the clearing at B-grade at the very least. I felt ready to take on anyone at the Grove.

Alex shrugged and patted Honey's firm neck again. 'Off you go, then. I'll call out instructions. You give it your best shot.'

I smiled to myself. I was going to do more than give it my best shot. I was going to leave Alex speechless. The Vovos would faint right there in the sand. Lena, Tash and Moll would cheer for us and Mrs S would have our names inscribed on the Honey and Ashleigh Honour Board for Brilliant Dressage Comebacks in ginormous gold letters. I couldn't wait to show everybody what we could do.

'Once I ring the bell you have forty-five seconds to enter the arena. Walk to X and halt to salute the judge. They'll be sitting at C.'

'No problem.' I gathered my reins, ordering my face to look confident and carefree, while inside my stomach was churning. I had to convince Alex that Honey was safe in the arena. This was our last chance.

Alex raised the bell and shook it. Honey didn't flinch. Her ears were forward and her head was high. She responded to the pressure of my legs on her sides and walked into the arena. I sighed, relieved. Honey had taken the first step.

I halted Honey at X and saluted the imaginary judge, holding both reins in my left hand, dropping my right hand to my side and bowing my head.

'Good, Ashleigh! Free walk to C, prepare for a working trot between C and H and trot from H to K. Halt her there and wait for instructions.'

I used the pressure of my legs to tell Honey to walk on and allowed her as much rein as she wanted. As we approached C, I had a brainwave. Anyone could do a working trot. That wasn't going to impress Alex one little bit. I was going to show him exactly what Honey could do. As she began the turn at C, I urged Honey into a trot and collected her. Her steps became shorter and lighter. I peeked quickly at Alex. He didn't look impressed yet. He looked confused. I wheeled Honey around in a circle. As I started her in another circle at H, I used my outside hand to stop her going on with the circle and my inside leg to keep her moving forward along the side of the arena. I looked straight ahead keeping my hips forward. A shoulder-in! We had done it.

'Whoa! Halt her now!'

Alex jogged into the arena. I pulled Honey up and he took hold of the reins under her chin.

'What was that?'

I bit my lip. Alex didn't look happy. He was supposed to be speechless. 'A shoulder-in?'

Alex frowned. 'I know what it was, I meant, what did you think you were doing? I gave you specific instructions and you didn't carry them out. How do you expect to pass dressage if you don't perform the test you're given?'

He was angry. I didn't know what to say. I looked over his head to Tash who, still mounted on Silver, shrugged. Brooke was cackling with Juliette.

'I don't know what you've been up to but I think you owe me an explanation.' Alex raised his hand. I don't know why. Maybe he was going to pat Honey. Maybe he was waving. All I know is that Honey suddenly seized up and tossed back her head, yanking the reins out of his hand. She backed out of the arena like a maniac, straight into the ring wall then shied violently. I wasn't ready for her — I thought all of that was behind us. I felt myself airborne for a moment then the air was whacked out of me as I hit the wall and fell to the ground. I couldn't breathe. I couldn't think. Everything hurt and, as I lay there on the sand watching her silver shoes flash in the sunlight centimetres from my face, I wasn't sure if I'd make it out of the ring at all.

I closed my eyes, wishing it was over, and didn't open them again until I heard someone calling my name. Alex (actually there were three Alexes) was looking down at me.

'Ashleigh,' he said. It sounded like he was talking underwater. 'Ashleigh, can you hear me?'

I couldn't speak. All I wanted to do was sleep. I closed my eyes again.

'Ashleigh, wake up!'

I couldn't open my eyes. Sleep was coming and I couldn't fight it. Someone slapped my hand but I didn't care.

'Tash!' Alex cried. 'Get Mrs Strickland in here NOW!'

That's all I remember. Sleep came and took me and I wasn't strong enough to argue.

SIXTEEN

Lena's Great Idea

'You gave us quite a fright, Miss Miller.' Mrs S sat on a chair beside my bed. I was alone in the cabin. I'd slept for hours, not even realising I'd been taken out of the ring on a stretcher. The Grove doctor had just left. It was shock, she'd said, that had made me sleep. No concussion, no breaks, no bleeding. But inky bruises had spread across my face, shoulder and hip where I'd hit the wall.

'Where's Honey? Is she all right? I want to see her!' I tried to sit up but I was really sore and lay back down on the bed.

'Miss Symon and Miss Bryant have had their

hands full all afternoon looking after her.' Mrs S smiled. 'There's nothing quite like good friends.'

The cabin door opened and Tash poked her head through. 'Can we come in?'

'Can they, please?' I pressed my hands together hopefully.

'Of course.'

Tash stepped through the door followed by Molly, who was balancing a tray piled high with food. Mrs S patted my good shoulder.

'I'm just going to ring your parents and give them an update. They're making their way here tonight to collect you.'

'No!' I cried.

Mrs S frowned. 'I don't understand.'

'I'm not leaving. The trials are only a week away. I want to stay. I want to do the final tests. I'm going to graduate.'

Mrs S frowned even deeper. 'Miss Miller, you've just had an incredibly lucky escape. I cannot allow you to take the trials. You're not fit and your horse is not reliable.'

I couldn't believe it. I was back where I'd started. I looked to Molly and Tash. Their faces said it all. I was the last person to know I'd be leaving the Grove. It wasn't fair!

'But Mrs Strickland, please!' I said. 'Please let me stay. It's only another week. I've come so far. Honey's worked so hard. If you could have only seen her in the clearing then you'd know what she can do. Please.' I wanted to cry. I imagined Brooke's face when she'd found out. I could see the Creepketeers in my head and hear their laughter ringing in my ears. I couldn't go home. I had to graduate.

'Tash?' I said, studying her face. 'Moll?'

My friends edged to my bed and sat down gingerly. They exchanged glances, each unwilling, it seemed, to be the first to speak.

'Maybe it's for the best,' Molly said. She was almost whispering.

'What?' I couldn't believe my ears. If anyone was going to be on my side it was Molly. And here she was sounding like a mini Mrs S. I grabbed Tash's hand, sure she wouldn't let me down.

Tash squeezed my fingers, but lowered her eyes.

'Not you, too!' I cried, snatching my hand back.

Tash squirmed. 'We've done all we can, Ash. Don't you get it?'

I heaved myself off the bed and regretted it immediately. My head throbbed like water was being pumped through it, in one ear and out the other with a few loop-the-loops in between. My sore muscles didn't appreciate it, either. Pain stabbed at my back, hip and ribs. I moaned and fell back onto the bed, pulling my pillow over my head.

'Ash,' Molly began. She touched my shoulder. I swatted at her hand.

'Go away.' Okay, so I was acting like a great big baby. But right then it seemed as though nothing in the world had ever been so unfair. Honey and I had worked so hard and it was all going to be taken away from us; graduation, the Honour Board, going home with something no other Shady Creek rider had ever achieved ... everything.

So what? said a little voice inside my head. *It's only Waratah Grove.* But the little voice was being drowned out by a louder, very angry voice bellowing like a cow stuck in the mud, the same words over and over: *NOT FAIR, NOT FAIR, NOT FAIR!*

Mrs S cleared her throat. 'It's time to go, girls. Miss Miller needs rest.'

The bed rocked gently as Tash and Molly got up.

'There's no use being angry with us, Ash.' Tash's voice was tight. 'We didn't throw you off or mess up Honey's head.'

'But you want me to give up,' I snarled into my pillow. 'And in my books that's just as bad.'

'Because we don't want to see you smashed up? Because we actually care what happens to you?' Tash was ranting. 'Well, sorry for wanting to see you leave the Grove in a car instead of an ambulance. Just get it into your head. You'll never be able to ride Honey in the arena.'

'Yes she will.' A small voice piped up from the lounge chairs.

I threw the pillow off my face and slowly sat up. 'Who was that? Who said that?'

Lena stood up, grinning, her two thick plaits a mess of straw and oddly coloured elastics. 'I did.'

'What did you mean?'

'Yeah.' Tash frowned. 'What did you mean?'

If it was possible, Lena's smile grew even bigger. 'I've got an idea. I think I can help you, Ash-a-leigh.'

Tash and Molly gaped at her. Mrs S smiled and nodded. 'Tell us your idea, Lena. We're all ears.'

★ ★ ★

My muscles ached and my head pounded but it wasn't enough to stop me following Lena and Biscuit to the dressage ring. First I'd managed to buy a little time by calling Mum and Dad and telling them I was fine. I promised to call again the next morning so that we could have the 'No Matter What You Say We Are Bringing You Home' conversation. Tash and Molly hurried along beside us, as eager as I was to hear what Lena had to say.

Lena pulled Biscuit up and patted her neck, beaming gappily at us.

'Ready, Freddy?'

'It's Ashleigh, actually.'

Lena giggled. 'I know that, silly.'

'I keep telling you, it's Ashleigh!' I fought to control the smile that was tugging at my lips.

Lena slapped at me playfully. 'You're funny.'

'No, I'm Ashleigh!'

'Cut it out!' Tash cried.

Molly muttered something about ten years. I put on my most serious face and looked expectantly at Lena. 'Could you show me . . . your idea?'

Lena's face burst into a rapturous smile. 'Of course, Ash-a-leigh!' Lena tugged gently on Biscuit's reins. The pony took a step forward. Lena led Biscuit for a minute or so then stopped abruptly. Biscuit halted. Lena patted her pony's neck, making soothing sounds. Biscuit took a step forward. Lena pushed her back. When Biscuit was standing perfectly still, in the same position she'd been in before she'd moved, Lena patted her again. Biscuit stood still and attentive. Lena tugged on her reins again and the pony moved forward. Lena repeated the process a few times. I looked on in a giddy mixture of confusion and awe.

'What on earth are you doing?'

Lena pulled Biscuit up and patted her neck, this time offering her a titbit from her pocket. 'I'm teaching her to park, Ash-a-leigh.'

'To *what*?' Molly, Tash and I cried in unison.

'To park. P-A-R-K.'

'Thanks for the spelling lesson,' Tash grumbled. Molly elbowed her sharply in the ribs.

Lena squeezed her eyes shut for a moment, concentrating hard. When she opened them again they were alight. 'You've got to teach Honey to do the same. You-you've got to teach her to stand still in the arena. You have to teach her that she moves when *you* tell her to move, not because she's scared or anything else.'

I was flabbergasted. 'That's it?'

Lena nodded deeply, slowly. 'That's it, Ash-a-leigh.'

'And you reckon this'll help Honey?'

'Pinky promise.' Lena offered me her pinky. I joined her, hooking my little finger around hers, and giving it a gentle shake.

'Pony pinky promise.'

Now we had a deal that couldn't be broken by anyone or anything. Ever.

'I'll get Honey.' I beamed at Lena. She grinned back.

Tash grabbed my arm. I winced. Lena and I untangled our pinkies.

'You're mad, Ash. If you bring Honey back in here you're off your rocker!'

I looked into Tash's eyes. 'Maybe I am. But I have to try.'

Tash's lips thinned out so much they almost disappeared. 'Maybe you need another knock on the head. Might clear your mind.'

I wondered for a moment whose side she was on. Didn't Tash want me to graduate? Didn't she want me to be on the Honour Board? A terrible feeling came over me. The words came out all by themselves.

'You don't want me to ride, do you? You want me to fail the Grove.'

'Ashleigh!' Molly gasped. Her hand flew to her mouth, which hung open in shock.

'It's true. Tash is scared. She's scared that I'm a better rider than her. She doesn't want anyone else to have a chance. She doesn't —'

Tash held up her hand. 'Save it, Ashleigh. I thought we were friends but . . . but you're more like her than you realise.'

I rubbed my forehead. Pain was banging rudely on my front door demanding to be let in. 'Like who?'

Tash regarded me through narrow eyes. 'Who do you reckon? Brooke. Go back to her, Ashleigh. You deserve each other.'

Tash turned on her heel and marched out of the arena. Molly looked from her to me, then followed Tash without looking back. Lena stared at the ground, scuffing the dust with the toe of her boot. Biscuit hung her head.

'Tash, wait!' I called. But it was too late. She was gone. I grabbed my head. I felt very strange.

'Don't worry, Ash-a-leigh, I'm still your friend.'

I gave Lena a weak smile. 'Thanks.'

'Do you wanna get Honey now?'

I nodded, unable to speak. My throat was tight and my eyes were hot. Lena understood. She understood a whole lot — that was for sure.

We walked to the stables together in silence. The terrible things I'd said to Tash spun around and around inside my head. My heart fell into my riding boots with a horrible splat.

Honey was in her stall. I was going to do this, but I would have to do it alone. I bridled Honey and stroked her nose. She looked at me sheepishly, guilt radiating from her sweet face.

'Don't worry, Honey,' I murmured. 'We're gonna fix this mess once and for all.' She rubbed her head on my shoulder and for a moment I thought everything would be all right. 'Together.'

SEVENTEEN

Jump Start

'How's your psycho horse?'

I didn't look up at Brooke but continued shovelling soggy cornflakes into my mouth. I had enough to worry about. Honey had steadfastly refused to park. Mum and Dad had steadfastly refused to believe that I wasn't in mortal peril when I spoke to them on the phone and Tash and Molly had been even more steadfast in their refusal to speak to, look at or come anywhere near me for two whole days. The last thing I needed was Brooke, snapping away at me like an angry goose.

'You're, like, so wasting your time on that nag.'

'Wasting your time,' Juliette droned.

Brooke picked up a spoon from the Roycroft table and stared at her reflection, smacking her painted pink lips together.

'How many days until the trials begin?' Brooke leaned close to me, cupping her ear with her hand. 'Five, did you say? Just five?'

Brooke stood up and patted my shoulder consolingly. 'Never mind, Ashleigh. There's always next year.'

'Next year.' Juliette nodded gravely.

I threw Juliette a withering look, wishing that if she was going to insult me she could at least think up something all by herself.

Brooke tipped back her head, laughing, and strutted from the dining hall, Juliette close on her heels, as usual, like a well-trained dog.

I slammed down my spoon and buried my head in my arms. What was happening here? Honey had started out well enough. Walking calmly into the arena. But she'd fidgeted so much, anxious to escape the arena, she looked more like she was tap-dancing than parking. We had a final jumping lesson ahead of us then a last run over the cross-country course and that was it. Next the trials. And our last chance to prove that we were Grove-worthy. I left the table just as Molly and Tash sat down, determined to make an early start in the stables. When I caught sight of them my heart squeezed, and I wanted to say something. But I had no choice, Tash and Molly would have to wait. Honey needed me and I had no time to lose.

Honey nickered when she saw me, her sweet golden head hanging over the stall door. If she'd had a watch on I'm sure she'd have tapped it impatiently.

I rummaged in my grooming kit and pulled out a body brush, zipping it over and over Honey's smooth, shiny coat and tried to ignore the aches all over my body that still lingered from my fall. I checked her legs and feet then threw her saddlecloth over her back, positioned it just right and settled her saddle down gently. I reached under her belly for the girth, sucking in my breath a little from the pain, and buckled it up tight, then gave each of her forelegs a good stretch.

By the time Honey was bridled and ready to go most of the stalls were a hive of pre-lesson activity. Strangely, there was very little chatter between the riders. Thinking they must all be as nervous as me about the trials, I grabbed hold of Honey's reins under her chin and opened the stall door, leading her out and into the waiting area and then down towards the jumping ring. I tried to block out my nerves and sore muscles, everything but the sound of my riding boots crunching and Honey's hooves clopping. I let the sounds run through my head, hoping they'd make me feel calm inside and out. When that didn't work, I thought about chocolate ice cream. No use. This was our last jumping lesson. Our last chance to perfect the course, to soak up as much from Joanne as we could, to convince ourselves that we were even in this league.

My heart pounded as I led Honey into the jumping ring. I could feel sweat, sticky on my face. Joanne nodded and smiled and I nodded back, stiff and tight, jamming my left foot into the stirrup and hauling myself, aching, into the saddle. I landed gingerly, feeling for my other stirrup and gathering my reins.

'Have you warmed up?' Joanne called, shielding her eyes against the morning sun.

I shook my head. 'Just about to.'

'Around the arena until she's limber, please. Walk to trot to gentle canter.'

I warmed up Honey seeing nothing but her ears and bouncing mane and the dirt on the ring floor. I squinted against the white stands, glinting gold in the sun, which warmed my face. It didn't take long for my nerves to wash away. It happened every time I rode. Nothing mattered except the horse, the sound of my heart beating along with her hooves and that feeling, that almost indescribable feeling, of being fused into one, closer than any two beings could or would ever be.

'Ashleigh, Ashleigh!'

'Huh?' I pulled Honey up, remembering where I was and walked her to the line of Roycrofts, who were waiting for their last jumping lesson. I scanned their faces quickly. Only Lena smiled. I squeezed into place beside her and concentrated on Joanne. No one, not Brooke, not Juliette and not even Tash, was going to ruin my chances at the Grove. I pushed at the huge lump that was rising in my throat at the thought of Tash and tangled my fingers in Honey's mane.

'Roycrofts, today is your last jumping lesson.' Joanne smiled at us, rubbing her hands together with what looked suspiciously like joy. 'You've worked hard over the last three and a bit weeks and it's time now to see what you can do. Today we'll be going over what we've learned one last time and jumping the course one last time before your trials. If you want to ask anything at all about the trials, now is the time to ask. Don't save your questions or worries for the marshalling area.'

Joanne tugged at her long braid and began a lengthy speech about balanced rhythm on the approach, in the air and on the landing, seats, posture and natural aids. Then she put us in order. We were jumping in our grades — Tash in A-grade; Molly, Lena and Juliette in B; Brooke and me in C. Brooke sent me a look. I screwed up my face into the nastiest expression I could muster and fixed it right back at her. She pointed at me and slammed a fist into her open palm. I pointed back at her and stuck my finger into my mouth, gagging.

'If you two ladies are all done, it's your turn.' Joanne was frowning so deeply her eyes had almost disappeared. I looked around, stunned. All the other Roycrofts had finished and were cooling out their horses.

'Brooke, you first.'

Brooke wiggled her eyebrows at me. I rolled my eyes right back. She lined Angel up and burst into a trot, quickening to a canter on Joanne's bell.

I watched Brooke. I'd never say it out loud, but she was good. She'd improved so much she may have even been better than C-grade. By the end of the course she'd clipped one rail, but none were down. I grimaced knowing how unbearable she'd be if I messed up. You have to do better, I ordered myself.

I moved into the starting position and gathered my reins. My stirrups were raised two notches and I was already leaning forward slightly. Honey's back arched — she was ready. Joanne rang the bell. My heels touched Honey's sides and she leapt into a gentle, rocking canter. I circled the ring once then pulled her head towards the first jump, sitting deeper in the saddle and squeezing my legs against Honey's sides. I put pressure on her mouth, enough to stop her speeding up. The fence was five metres away, three, two … Honey sank slightly then pushed off and soared, landing clear and straight into the canter. We cleared the second jump and the third and just as the daydream, so delicious, fogged up my head I heard a crack. Honey lurched. She landed heavily. There was a clunk of wood hitting wood and I knew. We'd knocked a rail down. Never mind, I thought. Only one jump. Only one rail. I focussed on the combination, but Brooke's laughter rang out and I lost concentration. Another clunk. Another rail. More laughter. Panic beat in my chest but I pressed on. Only three jumps to go. Clunk. Clunk. Clunk.

I slowed Honey from a canter to a trot, then walked her to Joanne. I was too ashamed to even look at her so I stared at the dirt in my fingernails.

Joanne was quiet for a minute. I could feel her eyes searching my face.

'What happened?' she said at last.

I shook my head and shrugged. I didn't know what to say. Brooke's kookaburra cackling echoed in my ears.

'Look at me,' Joanne said.

I stared at my pommel.

'I said, look at me.' There was something about her tone that told me she wasn't going to be ignored. My eyes met hers.

'You can do this.' Joanne poked my leg. One poke for every word. 'You can do this. You've done it before and you'll do it again and before you say anything I do NOT want to hear the word "can't"!'

I nodded, shaking my feet out of my stirrups and sliding to the ground. 'I have to cool her out.'

Joanne patted my shoulder and grinned. 'Just remember what I said.'

I nodded again, pulling Honey's reins over her head, clutching them under her chin. I wanted to believe Joanne. More than anything. But the tiniest bit of pressure and I'd cracked into little pieces and fallen apart. Grovers weren't supposed to crack under pressure. I led Honey to the warm-up arena to begin her cool down. Whatever had gone wrong out there, one thing was certain. I couldn't let it happen again. I led Honey in circles, cooling her out, trying in vain to switch off the voice in my head that was telling me that it should have been Becky here and not me. I was out of my league and nobody could help me.

EIGHTEEN

The Final Countdown

Honey worked hard in our final cross-country lesson, like I knew she would. The next day we were banned from the dressage ring yet again so I spent the lesson trying once more to teach her to park. Just when I'd started to think it would never happen, in the safety of the warm-up ring she finally got it. It was just as Lena said it would be. I halted Honey. She took a step forward, I pushed her back. She took a step back, I moved her forward. She took a step to the side, I brought her back again. Again and again until, finally, she stood still, watching me, her ears pricked forward, ready to go on my command and only on my command. I praised her, hugged her and kissed her face. She had done it! I had to try it in the dressage ring. I had to know.

The Roycrofts filed out of the lesson and into the warm-up ring for their cool down. I led Honey to the dressage ring. Alex was there, scribbling notes in his folder. He looked up at the sound of Honey's gentle snort. His eyes darkened.

'You shouldn't be here. You know that.'

I was ready. I'd already rehearsed my speech.

'I know. And I don't want to get into trouble, or get you into trouble.'

Alex frowned, but said nothing.

'I have to show you something. I just want you to watch.' I held my hands together, praying. He had to let us try. He just had to!

Alex frowned harder then rubbed his forehead. 'Do you have any idea how much trouble I'll be in if you get hurt again?'

'Yes,' I said quickly. 'But I won't. Coz Honey's changed. She can do it. I promise.'

I bit at my bottom lip, desperate, nerves tingling right through my body.

Alex's face softened slightly and he rolled his eyes. 'Okay,' he said gruffly. 'Just be careful.'

'You're the best!' I cried. Honey flinched. I settled her at once.

'I don't know about that,' Alex muttered. 'But, I'll be here. In case you need me.'

I wanted to kiss him. 'Thanks heaps!'

Alex waved me off and I led Honey into the arena. She stepped carefully beside me, step after step until we were inside the arena, standing on the very spot where she'd lost it. I stood still and faced her, head on. She stood watching me, waiting. I stroked her nose over and over, telling her what a good girl she was and how much I loved her for being so brave. She nuzzled my hands and I reached into the back pocket of my jeans, pulling out a slice of carrot I'd swiped from the kitchen. Honey accepted it and crunched contentedly. She was calm. For the first time in weeks she was calm in the arena.

I tugged her reins and took a step forward. Honey followed. I stopped and she stopped. I moved forward again, and again she followed me. We stopped. I led her around the arena, slipping her slices of carrot, praising her over and over. I stopped again. She stopped and stood still.

I pulled Honey's reins over her head and gathered

them at the pommel, clasping it and jamming my foot into the stirrup. I sprang into the saddle, my heart thumping, and settled my seat, praying that Honey would remain calm. She stood still and alert. Her breathing was easy and her muscles were relaxed. I gave her the command to walk on which she did. We rode once around the arena, then twice. Then again at a trot and completed a serpentine at the canter. All the while Honey was calm. I applied pressure on her mouth with the reins and she halted, standing as still and perfect as she had before. I felt weak with relief. She had done it! She'd been through so much, so much pain and fear. But she had put her trust in me and we'd come through it together.

I looked to Alex. He was on his feet, clapping, a grin spreading across his face.

I wrapped my arms around Honey's neck and breathed her in. She was so good, so brave. Warm tears ran down my face. My horse had given all she had, she had trampled on her fear and I knew she'd done it because she loved me. In that instant I knew that nothing else mattered. Not the trials, not Brooke, not even Tash and Molly. Nothing else mattered because I had the love of a horse and I loved her right back. What could be better than that?

'Mr George tells me he's decided to let you take your dressage test.'

I looked up from Honey's hoof, letting her foot drop gently back to the floor. Mrs S was peering over the wall of Honey's stall, smiling at me.

I straightened up, stretching my back, a grin tugging at my cheeks. 'He's the best.'

Mrs S nodded. 'I can't argue with that. I have to say, you've come a long way with that mare of yours. There aren't too many riders who could tackle a problem like Honey's and find a solution. I hope you understand what a wonderful young equestrian you are, not to mention those friends of yours. Miss Symon spent hours training with you and Miss Jones's idea was certainly a useful one.'

The smile was wiped from my face. How could I have been so mean to Tash? After everything she'd done for me. She'd given up her time to help me when she could have been riding Silver or just been with him. She'd passed up trail rides, free time, meals. She was the one who'd found out the truth about Honey's past. She was the one who'd helped me, helped Honey and me both. I felt sick. There was an ache in my chest. My head started to pound. I sank to the floor of Honey's stall, right beside a huge pile of her handiwork. Yep. I felt a lot like that.

'Miss Miller? Is everything all right?' Mrs S craned over the stall, looking down at me.

I shook my head. 'No. But I'm going to make it right.'

'Thatta girl.'

Her footsteps echoed down the aisle and I was left alone with my thoughts and that yucky sick feeling. And there was only one thing that would ever make it better.

The Roycroft table was quiet that night at dinner. In fact the whole dining hall was quiet. Nobody wanted to admit it but the trials were making everyone stressed. Mrs S's speech about the order of the day hadn't helped a bit. It had only served to remind everyone that the trials were happening whether we wanted them to or not. Dressage was up first, as was the tradition in eventing, followed by jumping the next day. The cross-country trials would take place the morning after, followed by the grooming and theory exams. We'd find out our total scores (and our fates) on Saturday, graduation day. I picked at my burrito, feeling like I would never want to eat again.

'Aren't you hungry, Ash-a-leigh?'

I smiled at Lena, who was stuffing forkfuls of burrito into her mouth one after the other, and shook my head. 'Nah.'

'By bot?' Lena mumbled through a mouthful.

I shrugged. 'Dunno. Just nervous, I guess.'

Lena swallowed hard. 'What about?'

She took a long sip of apple juice, staring at me with huge eyes. It was great having her to talk to, but it wasn't the same as having Tash and Molly. They were huddled together at the far end of the table. Every part of me wanted to be there with them. I watched them, my heart aching. Brooke sent me a slippery look, enjoying every minute of my unhappiness. I pushed my plate away. Enough was enough. I didn't know how much longer I could go on sleeping in a room full of people who weren't talking to me.

'I'm nervous about tomorrow, Lenes. The start of the trials. Aren't you worried?' I ripped my paper serviette into tiny pieces.

'I'm not worried,' Lena said simply, carving out another forkful of food. 'It's only horse riding.' She pushed the fork into her mouth and grinned.

I felt like I'd been hit in the head by a thunderbolt. The kid was a genius. It *was* only horse riding! I'd been a rider for as long as I could remember. I lived to ride. I rode to live. Honey and I would take the trials. And whether or not we passed, whether or not Tash and Molly were my friends, whether or not we were out of our league, we'd be okay because we'd be out there together.

NINETEEN

The Deal

I woke up early after a restless night's sleep. The dressage tests were on today. I dressed quickly and crept towards the cabin door. The Roycrofts slept on in a tangle of blankets and limbs flopping out from underneath lopsided doonas. Gentle snoring was coming from Kylie's room so it looked like the only person who'd had a sleepless night was me.

The sun was rising and thin fingers of light were creeping across the courtyard. My boots crunched as I made my way down to the stables, each footstep ringing out into the dawn. The air was moist and fresh and made my face tingle. Although the human Grovers were mostly still sleeping, the animals had clocked on for the day. Somewhere behind the stables a rooster was crowing. Cows mooed and horses whinnied to one another. One of the farm dogs trotted across the courtyard and parrots shrieked at the rising sun. I wondered why I'd never bothered to get up so early before.

At the stables Rex greeted me with a cheerful 'Morning' and went about his chores. Honey was waiting for me in her stall. She nickered loudly when she saw me, tossing her head.

I ran my hand down her face, then scratched at that other special place she liked so much just under her forelock.

'It's so good to see you, Hon,' I murmured. 'My best girl. Best horse ever.'

I let myself into her stall and filled her feed bin, scrubbed her water trough and mucked out. Being busy made me feel instantly calmer. And it gave me time to think. I ran through the test over and over in my head and tried to remember every word Mrs S had ever uttered in Equitation.

When Honey's stall was sparkling like a brand-new bit, I groomed her, running my hands carefully over her body and down each of her legs.

There were no lumps or swellings, no tenderness and no heat. Honey was fit to ride and ready for anything.

'Enjoy your brekkie, girl,' I said, letting myself out again.

'I, like, so can't believe that you talk to your horse.'

I groaned. 'What d'you want now, Brooke?'

Brooke took a step towards me. She was dressed in her usual pink and white riding ensemble. Her dark curls were pulled back tightly into a severe bun at the base of her neck. Her green eyes took me in. 'We need to talk.'

I shook my head. 'No, we don't.'

As I went to pass her she grabbed my arm, squeezing hard enough to hurt.

'When I say I wanna talk, you talk.'

I yanked my arm and she let me go.

'We need to, like, strike a deal.' Brooke folded her arms across her chest. 'Winner takes all.'

I folded my arms right back at her. 'What kind of deal?'

'Honour Board.'

My heart tweaked. 'What?'

'We're doing the trials, we're getting a final score. The person with the best score goes on the Honour Board, the person with the worst doesn't.'

'Everybody who passes goes on. You know that.'

Brooke laughed softly. 'You don't get it. I should have known you'd have trouble, like, getting your head around this.' She grabbed my arm again. 'Now listen. The trials are about two people, Miller, you and me. You get a better final score than me and I'll refuse to go on the Honour Board. I get a better score than you and you refuse. It's that simple.'

'That's sick!' I cried. 'Why? Why do you want to do this?'

Brooke shrugged. 'I don't want your name and mine on the same Honour Board.'

'But why?' I couldn't believe what I was hearing. Could she really hate me that much?

'Simple, I hate you.' Brooke's eyes flashed.

Yes, I guess she could.

'So, do we, like, have a deal?'

I don't know what came over me but I grabbed her hand and shook it as quickly as I could. As much as I was aching to see my name written on the Honour Board, just like so many amazing riders who had been at the Grove before me, as much as I wanted future Grovers to look up and see my name and say, 'Wow, Ashleigh Miller came to the Grove,' the feeling was totally mutual. I would rather miss out all together than see my name up there with Brooke's. Of course, we still had to take the trials and graduate.

Brooke sneered at me, satisfied with the outcome of our 'talk'. I had to get away from her. I took one last look at Honey over my shoulder and bolted for the door like a thirsty pony for a water trough.

Despite having eaten what seemed to be the most stable breakfast on offer — a piece of toast and jam with a glass of apple juice — my stomach churned. I'd never felt anything like this before. My whole body was cold. Sweat beaded on my forehead and trickled down my sides and back. I shook so hard my teeth chattered. I was totally, deathly afraid.

Dressage. I had fought so hard to be allowed to take the test and now that it was upon me all I wanted to do was throw up. I had tried to push the sick feeling out of my body (thankfully not out through my mouth) during my warm-up, but it was still there, deep in the pit of my stomach like a big yucky bowling ball.

The dressage tests were being held in stages, Preliminary through to Advanced, which meant that Molly and I were up first and everyone else at the Grove was going to watch us. A small part of me couldn't wait for it to be over. The rest of me wanted to pack my saddlebags and skip town, never to return.

I'd never done a dressage test before, not to mention I hadn't finished even one of Alex's lessons. I'd memorised the test but had only had time to practise it with Honey once or twice. Alex had often said that a horse shouldn't know a test off by heart — that the horse should respond to the rider's commands and not just go through the motions. One thing was for sure. Unless Honey had stayed up all night cramming, she was going to have to respond to my commands. She didn't have any other option.

Molly Bryant was called first. I caught her eyes for just a moment. She looked as terrified as I felt. I offered her a small good luck smile. She nodded slightly and hit the ring, starting by saluting the judges — Mrs S, Alex and a man I didn't recognise — then launched into the test. I watched her, dressed in her finest riding outfit, totally focussed on Rebel and the test. For a moment I was able to forget my own fear. Then, just as quickly as it had started, Molly's test was over. The Grovers applauded loudly, Tash whistling and chanting, 'Go, Molly!' The judges scribbled on their papers for a few minutes then Mrs S switched on a microphone.

'Ashleigh Miller.'

'Oh, no!' My hand flew to my mouth. It was time. I squeezed my eyes shut tight, rolling the name of each of the twelve movements down behind my eyelids like movie credits.

'Psst.'

I opened my eyes. A Hoy girl with long red hair was waving at me frantically.

'Get a move on! They'll disqualify you!'

I gathered my reins and entered the arena at A. Honey was calm. I walked to X, halted and saluted the judges. What was next? A working trot to C, then track left. I nudged Honey into a trot and the test had begun. The stands were silent. My heart pounded and my hands were sweating. I gripped my reins hard, trying to remember to breathe. We reached C, the end of the arena, and I shifted my weight left, just slightly, moving my left leg back and applying gentle pressure to the reins. We had to work together. We had to perform seamlessly. It had to look like I wasn't doing anything, that Honey was receiving my commands telepathically and obeying them without hesitation.

Honey turned left and I sighed with relief. We had managed a movement. Only eleven to go.

I balanced my weight and maintained pressure on Honey's sides and she continued down the side of the arena at a working trot, H to E then E to K. I knew what was coming up and that it would be one of the trickiest movements of the entire test. I knew Honey was being marked on her impulsion — how well she was moving forward — and that her impulsion depended one hundred per cent on me and my commands. I prepared myself, looking ahead at the markers. Just as we approached A, Honey responded to my signals and moved into a working canter. I had to fight myself not to praise her aloud. There would be time for that afterwards. Right now we had to concentrate.

We cantered to B. Honey held her head up, her ears forward. Her feet beat against the sand. I was so proud to be riding her. I had never felt safer, never felt so much at home in the saddle as I did just then. My heart swelled, full of love for this horse. She had conquered so much fear to please me.

I applied pressure to her mouth and she returned to the trot at B, we circled left again and continued to trot to H, then cut diagonally across the arena from H to X. It was then I realised my mistake. I pulled Honey up sharply. We should have been walking! It was awful. Honey tossed her head and halted for a moment. I could hear rumbling in the stands and imagined a lot of it was coming from Brooke. It was only the first phase of the trials and she was probably already celebrating. I glanced quickly at Alex, my heart beating hard. He made a 'move on' signal with his hands, so I nudged Honey into a walk.

I changed my weight and used my aids until Honey turned right. I tried not to worry about the mistake but I was shaken. All I wanted right then was for it to be over. The list of movements ticked over in my mind and apart from a left turn at G that should have been a right, we got to the end in one piece. I brought Honey to a halt at X, the very centre of the arena and saluted the judges. As I raised my head I heard something coming from the stands that sounded like rain. It took a moment for me to realise that it was applause. For me and Honey! I beamed out at the crowd of Grovers from underneath my riding helmet, our achievement dawning on me for the first time. After all we'd gone through, after all the extra training and begging and hoping we had done it. We'd performed our very first dressage test together and no matter what the score, I felt like a winner.

I scanned the faces of the Grovers, finally finding the one person I needed to share the moment with. Tash smiled down at me, clapping. I grinned back at her. I owed her so much. She gave me the thumbs up. It was one of the sweetest moments ever.

TWENTY

Horse Trials

'Brooke really said that?' Molly said, staring at me with round eyes. Tash shook her head slowly. I had spilled the whole story from start to finish. We were sitting under a tree watching our horses munch on the sweet green grass in the day paddock. Honey and Rebel were standing nose to nose as usual. Silver was rolling, a look of pure ecstasy on his face.

I nodded. 'You bet your bridle.'

'Wow.' Tash waved at a fly. 'Then there's only one thing for you to do.'

'I know. Beat her.' I rubbed my forehead the way I always do when I'm stressed.

'What's up?'

'It's easier said than done.'

Molly and Tash shrugged. 'Nah.'

I smiled at them. They were great friends. We'd talked for ages after the dressage tests, apologising over and over for how awful we'd been to each other. It made my stomach ache to think how much time we'd wasted. There were only two whole days to go until our parents would be here to pick us up. We'd never have this time here again. I couldn't believe we'd spent so much of it being mad at each other.

'How did Brooke go in dressage?' I asked. 'I couldn't bear to watch.'

Tash and Molly exchanged glances.

'She did well,' Tash said. 'She's a champion, after all.'

'But there's still jumping and you're the best in Roycroft at cross-country,' Molly added.

'I guess,' I said, feeling no better.

The next day, Honey was warmed up and ready to go. She was alert, watching and listening, her ears flicking back and forth. I patted her neck, trying to focus on my breathing as we cantered our circles around and around the warm-up ring. A practice jump had been set up for us as part of our warm-up and we sailed over it again and again.

One by one the Roycrofts were called and bit by bit the ring emptied. We were jumping in our grades, which meant that for the first time Brooke and I were riding head to head. Although I knew I had a better chance of a good result in jumping than I did in dressage, I was even more nervous than yesterday. If Brooke beat me here, she would beat me fair and square. My heart fluttered.

I tried to tell myself that the only thing that mattered now was riding — riding the very best I could. Not even beating Brooke mattered, not really. The problem was, it did matter. It mattered a whole lot. I shook my head, trying to clear out all the scary thoughts that rattled my brain. Just get out there and jump well, I ordered myself. That will be enough for you. It was a beautiful theory.

Before long, only Brooke and I were left, and then Honey and I were alone.

'Ashleigh Miller.' Joanne's voice floated out over the loudspeaker.

It was time.

I walked Honey into the jumping ring, holding my reins so tightly my fingernails were cutting into the palms of my hands. I could hear the distant rumble of the Grovers in the grandstand. I glanced quickly at the judges' table and saw Joanne, Mrs S and the same man who'd judged dressage. I saluted them and urged Honey into a canter around and in between the six fences. I'd walked the course and knew which jump I had to start from. I told myself to relax.

I heard the bell. I had thirty seconds to start. Honey tensed. I gathered my reins and pulled her towards the first jump. It was a straight fence made from four planks painted red and white with sloping wings on each side. Honey cantered a few steps and it was upon us. I sat deep in the saddle and leaned forward, applying pressure to Honey's sides, holding my reins short and my hands low. Honey stretched her neck, lowering her head, preparing herself, then took off, tucking her forelegs up and pushing off with her hind legs. She stretched her neck out further still, gathering her hind legs up under her body as she sailed over the jump before raising her head slightly, stretching out her forelegs and touching down.

I pulled her to the left and over a spread fence then prepared her for the combination: two straight fences painted brightly in a mix of red, blue and white. The first disappeared underneath us followed quickly by the second. Honey seemed to have taken over. I was merely a passenger on her back. She was showing me how it was done, stretching and soaring and stretching and soaring, each time landing light on the other side and straight into the canter, only needing me to steer her.

A grey brick wall with a white pole on top sat close behind. Again I prepared Honey. She stretched out and pushed off. I moved my hands up her neck, leaning forward, while sitting deep. I looked down and saw the arena floor and the jump underneath us then, just as I looked ahead to the next jump, I heard a clunk. There was no denying it, the terrible sound of horseshoe hitting timber. I glanced over my shoulder in time to see the white pole topple and fall. My heart sank with it. Honey touched down and I looked forward again, pulling her to the right for the fifth fence, a single oxer — one pole suspended between two stands. We cleared it. Maybe we still had a chance.

A second combination of two straight fences melted away beneath us followed by another spread fence.

We reached the final fence. Honey was tiring. It had been a long day. It had been a long four weeks! I struggled to focus. Honey cantered towards the fence, a double oxer with two sloping wings and a 'V' shape underneath the poles emblazoned with the Waratah Grove crest in blue and white. This was our last chance. We'd picked up four penalty points for the brick wall. I wanted to finish on a clean jump. I balanced in the saddle, settling right in. Honey began to stretch and I leaned forward. The rest happened so fast. She took off, soared and stretched out, touching down and cantering away to the finish. I pulled her clear of the course to a trot and then a walk. The crowd applauded. I looked to the judges' table. Joanne gave me a wink, Mrs S clapped. I patted Honey's damp neck, breathing hard. Two down, one to go.

TWENTY-ONE
Easy Rider

'Ready for cross-country?' Tash pulled on her boots, her wild hair frizzing out all over her head.

It was Friday, our final trial was here and everybody was excited. And a little scared.

'Ready as I'll ever be.' I tucked my shirt inside my joddies and examined my reflection in the mirror. A kid in riding clothes, a freckly nose and a ponytail looked back at me.

'This'll be easy for you, Ash,' Molly said. 'If I close my eyes I can still see you and Honey flying over those jumps at the Champs. You guys are an awesome team.'

'Just like you and Rebel,' I said, putting my arm around her shoulder. 'And Tash and Silver, of course.'

'Of course!' Tash laughed as she wrestled her hair into an elastic band.

'Will you losers cut it out. You're, like, making me wanna spew.' Brooke pushed her way to the mirror and leaned in close. She rubbed pink lipstick on her lips then turned to me. 'Don't forget our little deal, Miller. Just keep riding the way you rode yesterday — I love to see my name in big gold letters.'

Brooke smacked her lips together and stalked out of the cabin, tailed by the ever-faithful Juliette.

'I don't know what you ever saw in her, Ash.' Molly shook her head.

I groaned. 'At least I won't have to see her any more after tomorrow.'

Tash frowned. 'I can't believe it's nearly over.'

'*Nearly* over,' Molly said. 'We still have the slight problem of a cross-country trial and grooming and theory exams.'

Tash and I clasped hands. Molly added hers.

'It's in the bag.' I pulled my two friends into a hug.

I waited in the cross-country marshalling area for my turn, my guts gurgling. Molly had already gone.

Brooke and Lena, too. It was just Tash, Juliette and me. I eyed off the competition. Juliette, who was slumped in the saddle, looked like she was having a nice relaxing day at the beach while Storm ambled around, keeping warm. Tash was trotting Silver in circles, muttering to herself and making the occasional fist in the air with one hand. I was out next. My heart raced. I stroked Honey's neck over and over.

'It's okay, girl,' I murmured, but I felt sick. Sicker than sick.

I closed my eyes and took deep, slow breaths, trying to clear my mind and calm my stomach.

'Are you ready? Are you okay?'

I opened my eyes. Kylie stood beside me with a clipboard and a stopwatch, panting. She'd spent the entire morning rushing from one Roycroft to another checking and re-checking tack, assessing horse fitness and fastening body protectors.

I started to shake. It was too much. The pressure, the Iced Vovos, going out there all over again and trying to prove myself — again. The whole thing was crashing down on me, like a monster wave. I was about to be rumbled, big time.

'I can't do it.' The words came out before I could stop them.

'What was that?'

I shook my head, shivering. 'I can't. I'm not good enough. It was all a mistake.'

'I can't believe what I'm hearing.' Kylie's face was red. 'Haven't you learnt anything here? Has being a Roycroft meant nothing to you?'

I licked my lips. They were dry. My tongue was dry. I tried to swallow a huge sticky wad of fear but it was lodged in my throat.

'Too hard,' I gasped. 'Go home.'

I was breathing fast, too fast. The marshalling area began to spin.

Kylie shook my leg. 'Ashleigh!'

I peeped at her, then rubbed my forehead hard. Honey snorted and shook her head.

'You're a Roycroft. That's very special,' Kylie said.

I raised my eyebrows. I didn't get it.

Kylie continued. 'Your assignment on the Roycroft family. What did you learn from that?'

I thought hard. Bill Roycroft.

'Rome Olympics,' I said softly.

Kylie patted my knee, her other hand on Honey's reins. 'What happened in Rome?'

'Bill Roycroft, he, he …' I began. 'He broke his collarbone but he kept on riding. He won the gold medal.'

Kylie smiled. 'He sure did.'

'Yeah,' I said. 'He did.'

'Well?'

I sat up straight, breathing in through my nose and out through my mouth. I thought about Honey, about the course, about Bill Roycroft and my parents and Gary Cho and Becky and my new friends and Mrs S. I thought about all the people who believed in me and Honey and suddenly I felt better.

'I'm a Roycroft.' The words had never meant so much.

'And?' Kylie was beaming.

'I'm ready.' I gathered my reins and nudged Honey.

'Good luck, Ash!' Tash called after me.

I turned around for a moment and waved to her, my fear melting away. She waved back and gave me the thumbs up.

'Now focus,' Kylie said once we were at the starting line. She patted my leg and I shook off my stirrup. She lifted my saddle flap to check I'd moved the stirrups up two notches. All was well. Kylie shoved my foot back into my stirrup. 'Relax and focus. You know what to do out there so let's see you do it.'

I smiled down at her. 'Thanks, Kylie.'

Kylie gave me a wink. 'Knock 'em dead.'

I waited for the bell. Honey's muscles tensed. The Grove fell quiet. I looked out at the course, at the long green stretch ahead of me. Mrs S, sitting in the judges' box, raised the bell. I gripped my reins. The bell rang out across the Grove and Honey burst across the starting line. Her hooves pounded against the straight. I could smell the grass and the tossed up mud. Shrubs, trees and the occasional spectator appeared and disappeared in an instant. We were flying.

The first jump was the log. Kylie's words ran through my head. Rhythm and balance, it was all about rhythm and balance. But most of all it was about trust. I trusted Honey and she'd proven that she trusted me. My hand dropped to her shoulder. I patted her for just a moment.

'We can do it, Honey,' I murmured.

My hands began to rise as we approached the jump. I kept my seat close to the saddle but raised my weight slightly. Honey stretched out her neck and head. I leaned forward. My hands followed. Honey pushed off and we soared. Her feet found the ground again and she cantered away.

Next came the fence, followed by the brush hut before we were galloping up the hill again towards the brick wall. I shifted my weight forward allowing Honey's hindquarters to power us ahead. The wall sat just at the top, looking down on us smugly. I sat deep, squeezing my legs, pushing Honey harder up and over. Balance and rhythm, I thought as Honey pushed off.

We began the gallop downhill. I kept my seat in the saddle, my weight down in my heels and my legs pushed forward slightly. The next obstacle was ahead, 10 metres, then 5, then I felt Honey leap again and we were clear.

The rest of the course was a blur of speed, jumps, turns, a spattering of spectators and green and then finally the last jump was in sight. The oxer. Honey cantered towards it, cleared it and galloped for home where Kylie and the Roycrofts were waiting. My heart sang with joy as I watched my friends jumping up and down, cheering and clapping. I threw my arms around Honey's damp neck, soaking my face with her sweat. It had all been worth it, just for this ride. The look on Brooke's face said it all. For the first time since we'd arrived at the Grove, I felt we'd earned the right to be here.

'Graduation tomorrow and then we're going home,' I whispered to my friends that night. I was snuggled up in bed in Roycroft cabin, Molly on one side of me, Tash on the other.

My heart was breaking. Never again would I fall asleep in this room, watching the dancing shadows on the ceiling. Never again would I hear the slow deep breathing of my roommates or open my eyes and see their faces. This was our last night together. I was aching for home, but at the same time not wanting to leave.

'I can't believe it's over,' Molly mumbled. She was half-asleep, exhausted. It had been a big day with the cross-country trials in the morning, the grooming and theory exams in the afternoon, and a gruelling cleanup of the cabin after dinner. It looked strange now, without our clothes everywhere and no photos taped to the walls.

'It's only just beginning, Moll,' Tash murmured. 'Right, Lena?'

Lena yawned. 'Uh-huh, Tasha.'

'Will you losers, like, shut your big mouths and go to sleep!'

I grinned. 'I'll miss you, Brookey!'

'Plug it!'

Strange as it sounded — it was probably exhaustion — I would miss her. But nothing like I'd miss Tash and Molly. My new friends. My best new friends. How was I going to survive without them?

TWENTY-TWO
Honour Bound

I sat in the dining hall wedged between Tash and Molly. Lena snuggled into Tash. The hall had never looked so grand. Gold and silver balloons bumped against the ceiling. The newest Honour Board had been taken down from the wall and was sitting on the stage. I could see the names of past Grovers inscribed in gold letters. A long table was weighed down with trophies. In pride of place was the Waratah Grove Cup.

Everyone was dressed in their finest riding clothes. Alex had scrubbed up for the occasion with a zinc-less face and Joanne and Kylie looked like they'd spent the morning at the hairdresser's. Mrs S was decked out in her green tartan knickerbockers and hat and Mr S was wearing his best belt buckle. My insides wriggled. Nobody knew their scores. Nobody knew whose names would be inscribed on the Honour Board. Nobody knew who'd leave with the greatest prize of all, the Waratah Grove Cup.

'I'm so scared,' Molly whispered.

'What for?' I said. 'You were brilliant. You'll make it for sure.'

'What about me?' Tash moaned. 'I totally messed up that last flying change. And my brain went into meltdown in the theory.'

'Will you guys relax?' I grabbed their hands, trying to push my own fear down. I had done my best. But what if it wasn't good enough? I didn't know if I could cope with knowing that Brooke's name would be on the Honour Board instead of mine. I shivered.

Mrs S cleared her throat.

'Welcome to graduation!'

Every single Grover burst into applause. Mrs S smiled down at us.

'This morning is the culmination of your stay at Waratah Grove. Each and every one of you should be proud of what you've achieved here. You arrived as riders. You are leaving as equestrians. You will go out into the world with the skills you developed here and the knowledge that no matter who you are or where you're from, you are Grovers. The Grove will unite you for the rest of your lives. And while I have grown fond of you all and am sorry to see you leave us, I am comforted by the fact that news of your future successes will reach me and that I will be as proud of you then as I am today.' Mrs S paused and pulled a white hanky from her pocket.

I squeezed my friends' hands. No matter how much Mrs S was going to miss us, I was going to miss them more. More than anything.

Mrs S cleared her throat again. 'Before we start … Parents?'

The door of the hall opened and the parents streamed in, clutching cameras. Some were waving. All were grinning. I stood up, searching. Where were they? I'd missed them so much. A huge belly entered the room followed closely by a frantic-looking man with red hair.

'Mum!' I cried. 'Mum, Dad!' I jumped up and down waving both hands above my head. Mum saw me and promptly burst into tears. Dad clutched at her wrist, feeling for her pulse.

'I can't believe your parents actually came back for you,' Brooke said, sneering.

'I can't believe yours actually found their way.' I fluttered my eyelashes at Brooke.

'If parents could please find a seat we'll continue,' Mrs S said, indicating chairs at the back of the hall. There was a scraping of chairs as the parents settled, and then a very distinct 'Helen, do you need to elevate your legs?', followed by silence.

Mrs S called Joanne to the stage. She looked really beautiful. From the look on Alex's face my guess was that he was thinking the same thing. Joanne made a short speech about the Hoy girls and then called each one to the stage. Mrs S presented them with a trophy, a certificate and a sealed envelope. Photos were taken, the Grovers applauded and they sat down again, admiring their trophies and comparing them with those of their friends before they ripped open their envelopes.

Alex was next, praising the Morgan boys for their hard work in the arenas and for keeping him on his toes. More trophies, more certificates, more envelopes, more photos. I squirmed in my seat.

'Finally, I would like to call Kylie Henry to the stage,' Mrs S said at last.

That was more like it! I sat up, my fingers crossed. Kylie smiled down at us.

'Roycroft girls,' she said. 'Each of you made Waratah Grove a joy. You've had your ups and downs, but you've given it your all and reminded me why I took up riding in the first place.'

Kylie picked up a trophy and handed it to Mrs S. 'Brooke Barnes.'

I rolled my eyes. Brooke stood up, ramming her knee into my back and marched up the stairs.

'Go, Brooke baby!' a woman shrieked from the back of the hall. Brooke collected her trophy then looked down at me, waving her envelope. I glared at her, hoping that dirty looks could do actual harm.

'Molly Bryant.'

'Go, Molly!' I said, squeezing her hand. Molly climbed the stairs, shook Mrs S's hand and accepted her trophy, certificate and envelope. She spotted her parents in the crowd and waved, beaming.

'Lena Jones.'

There was a gasp from the parents as tiny Lena climbed the stairs. The trophy was almost as big as she was.

'Ashleigh Miller.'

'Oh, wow!' I wheezed. I scrambled out of my chair and up the stairs. Kylie handed my trophy to Mrs S who grabbed my hand and pumped it before handing it to me. I read the inscription. Mrs S pushed a certificate and an envelope into my other hand. A flash went off and I stepped back, joining Molly and Lena.

Juliette was called, then Tash, and we posed for a group photo. The hall erupted in cheers and applause. I held my trophy above my head. We had made it.

'We have one more prize to award,' Mrs S said as the Roycrofts found their seats. 'The Waratah Grove Cup.'

I sucked in my breath. From the sound of it, so did everyone else.

'On your first day I told you about the Cup and the kind of rider it takes to win it. The Waratah Grove Cup hasn't been awarded for six months, but I am delighted to inform you that your instructors and I reached a unanimous decision.'

I nudged Tash and Molly. We all crossed our fingers. I crossed my legs, toes and my eyes, for extra luck.

'Would Molly Bryant come forward?' Mrs S peered out at the Grovers.

'Moll!' I gasped. 'Congrats!'

Tash pulled her into a hug. Molly's mouth hung open.

'Go!' I said. 'You won, Moll. You did it!'

Molly walked up the stairs, a look of complete shock on her face. She accepted the Waratah Grove Cup, shook Mrs S's hand and beamed. I stood up, clapping. Tash did likewise, then Lena was on her feet.

'Go, Molly!' I cheered. I was so happy for her. Nobody deserved that Cup more than Molly.

It wasn't long before everyone in the room — except the Iced Vovos, of course — was on their feet, cheering for Molly. I felt like a winner, too.

We were graduates of Waratah Grove and nobody could ever take that away from us.

'So, did you beat her?' Tash grinned at me, waving her envelope. She'd graduated top of the class. But nobody was surprised about that.

I grinned right back. 'Course I did. Only by two points, though.'

Molly high-fived me. 'So does this mean she's off the Honour Board? After all, a bet's a bet.'

I laughed. 'Are you kidding? She got amnesia the second she saw my score.'

'Typical,' Tash said. 'Still, if it hadn't been for old Brookey we may not have become friends.'

We were silent for a moment.

'I guess this is goodbye.' Molly grabbed my hand.

'No, Moll,' I said. 'It's not goodbye.'

Tash slipped her arms around our shoulders. 'It's more like, "See you real soon".'

Earlier that day, we'd held a friendship ceremony under our tree by the day paddock vowing to be friends forever. Each of us had signed our names on a piece of paper. Then we'd buried it under the tree. We'd be back again one day and we'd dig it up together.

I had so much to say to them, but my throat was tight. The aching in my chest wasn't making it any easier.

'Ashleigh!'

I looked over my shoulder. Dad was standing by

the car waving to me and pointing at his watch. It was time to go. With Mum and her bladder I'm sure we'd be stopping at every petrol station we passed the whole way home. Honey was already in the Chos' float and the car was packed. I'd said goodbye and thank you to Mr and Mrs S, Rex, Kylie, Alex and Joanne. I'd hugged Lena and promised to write. I'd even blown the Iced Vovos a kiss. I won't say what they blew back.

I drew Tash and Molly into a tight hug, not wanting to let them go. Tears spilled down my face.

'I'm going to miss you guys,' I said. It was all I could manage. They hugged me back. Molly was crying too.

I broke away, turned and ran. Dad's arms were waiting. I fell into a cuddle. But before we left I needed one last look. There they were, waving. Molly with her sweet round face and Tash with those teddy bear ears.

'Goodbye!' I yelled. 'Bye!'

I slid into the back seat behind Mum, closed the car door and wound down the window. Dad started the engine. Molly and Tash waved, their arms around each other.

'Looks like you made some friends,' Mum said as the car rolled slowly out of the gate. The float bounced along behind us. I could see Honey through the window tearing at her haynet.

'I sure did.' I waved back at them until I couldn't see them any more. Then I slumped into the seat, already missing them so much.

'Speaking of friends, Becky can't wait to see you.' Mum twisted around — as much as she could manage — and gave me a smile.

'How is she?' I said. 'And Jenna, how's Jenna?'

'One thing at a time.' Dad laughed. 'We should have made the most of the peace and quiet, Helen.'

'Dad!'

'There is some news I think you'll be interested in,' Mum said.

'Is it about the baby?' I wanted to tell them how much I wanted the baby, too. About how I realised there was enough room in our house and our hearts.

'Not this time — this is horsy news.'

I raised my eyebrows. 'Since when do you hear horsy news?'

'Since I met the owner of Shady Trails at the bakery and she just happened to mention that she needed expert riders to work for her and I just happened to mention that I knew a very expert rider called Ashleigh Miller.'

'Shady Trails? What are you talking about?'

Dad looked over his shoulder. 'It's a new riding school. It's opening up soon.'

I was gobsmacked. 'Where? How?'

'Honey's old owners sold up their place at last and the new owners have been busy building and renovating.'

A new riding school in Shady Creek!

I looked out of the window as we drove further away from Waratah Grove. It was so great to be going home. I just knew there were more adventures to come and new friends to make. And I couldn't wait to meet them all.

Acknowledgements

I would like to thank my publisher at HarperCollins, Lisa Berryman, my editor Lydia Papandrea and my agent Jacinta DiMase for their wonderful encouragement and guidance. Thank you to my beautiful kids — Mariana, John and Simon. To Seb, my best friend, I love you. Thank you to my ever-supportive family — Mum, Dad, Andy, Cassandra, Mike, Hayley, Kaitlin and Caleb — and my friends.

The Publisher and Author would like to thank all those involved with the cover: Photographer, Belinda Taylor (www.bellaphotoart.com.au); Models, Gabriella Power (Ashleigh, front and back cover) and Annika Blau (Jenna, back cover); Cash and Cash's owner, Grahame Ware Jr (www.livestockforfilms.com.au); and Horseland Artarmon, NSW (www.horseland.com.au) who supplied the clothing.

Photo by Dyan Hallworth

KATHY HELIDONIOTIS lives in Sydney and divides her time between writing stories, reading good books, teaching and looking after her three gorgeous children. Kathy has had ten children's books published so far. *Horse Mad Academy* is the third book in the popular Horse Mad series. Watch out for Book 4, *Horse Mad Heroes*, coming soon.

Visit Kathy at her website:

www.kathyhelidoniotis.com